# Killer in the Carriage House

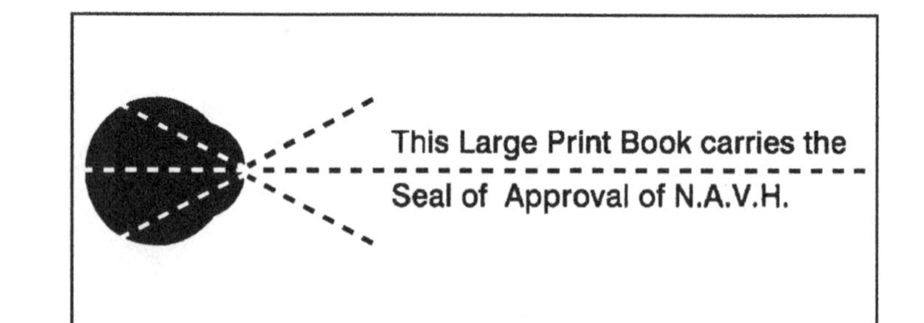
This Large Print Book carries the
Seal of Approval of N.A.V.H.

A VICTORIAN VILLAGE MYSTERY

# KILLER IN THE CARRIAGE HOUSE

SHEILA CONNOLLY

**THORNDIKE PRESS**
A part of Gale, a Cengage Company

Farmington Hills, Mich • San Francisco • New York • Waterville, Maine
Meriden, Conn • Mason, Ohio • Chicago

Thorndike Press, a part of Gale, a Cengage Company.


Thorndike Press® Large Print Mystery.
The text of this Large Print edition is unabridged.
Other aspects of the book may vary from the original edition.
Set in 16 pt. Plantin.

**LIBRARY OF CONGRESS CIP DATA ON FILE.**
**CATALOGUING IN PUBLICATION FOR THIS BOOK**
**IS AVAILABLE FROM THE LIBRARY OF CONGRESS**

ISBN-13: 978-1-4328-7181-9 (hardcover alk. paper)

Published in 2019 by arrangement with Macmillan Publishing Group LLC/St Martin's Publishing Group

Printed in Mexico
1 2 3 4 5 6 7 23 22 21 20 19

There is one person who more than
any other provided the inspiration
and the model for this book:
my great-great-grandfather,
Silas Abbott Barton.

I never knew him, but I know a lot about him. He signed up a soldier in the Civil War when he was sixteen (and spent the war bravely defending Boston Harbor without firing a shot at anyone); he opened a small art gallery; he brought electricity to the city of Lynn, Massachusetts; he ran in a congressional primary (and lost); he was part of the founding of Thomson-Houston Electric Company, and stayed on when it merged with Thomas Edison's company to form the General Electric Company; he must have gotten bored, because he left GE and purchased the Waltham Watch Tool

Company (which did not make watches, but made the tools to make watches, for which Waltham is famous).

He remodeled an old farmhouse in Waltham and turned it into a handsome Victorian building (it was rumored that no two doorknobs in the house were the same) for his wife and only child. For a genealogist he is a treasure trove, and I've given him an important role in the Victorian Village Mysteries.

# ACKNOWLEDGMENTS

When I started writing this book, I had a mental picture of two small towns that I knew personally. One was a town where I grew up, and while it was not far from New York City, it had changed surprisingly little over a couple of centuries. The other was Boonsboro, Maryland, where Nora Roberts has a small bookstore. I was invited to be part of a signing there, and in my spare time I wandered around the town and looked at details. The bottom line is that both towns, however far apart in distance and in time, have preserved the original layout and buildings, hidden under a layer of modern siding or plaster or paint.

I should also acknowledge that a small part of the inspiration for this series was the fact that the town where I now live decided a few years ago to purchase a historic eighteenth-century house on the outskirts of the town. It was built by a then-prominent industrialist for his son, who married the state governor's daughter. Purchasing the site required a public vote, which passed comfortably (which I guess means that as a resident I own a minuscule percentage of the place), and the house and grounds are now open to the public. If this town could do it, I could certainly create a fictional town to do the same thing.

One thing that is delightful about picturing fictional Asheboro in the post–Civil War era is the collision of past and present that is evident. While it was and remains a sleepy little town, like so many places in the later nineteenth century it faced problems with transportation, employment, modernization, and more. That's why Kate was called in to help, but she has a vision for the town. What would happen if you tried to revive a town that time had passed by? That's what my heroine Kate Hamilton tries to do, although finding a murder victim gets in the way now and then.

Once I had my setting I needed a long-empty mansion as the focus of the town's revival. Luckily my great-great-grandfather provided me with one. It's still standing, although all the elegance has been stripped from both the exterior and the interior. But a model for the interior can be found in the luscious Tiffany interiors of the Mark Twain House in Hartford, Connecticut. In addition, I live in an 1870 Victorian house. While it is nowhere near as large and opulent as the mansion in the series, it provides me with a wealth of details of how houses of that era were designed and built.

I owe many thanks to my tireless agent, Jessica Faust of BookEnds, who put me together at a conference with Hannah Braaten, editor at St. Martin's. That publishing house was new to me then, and it has been a pleasure getting to know Hannah and the rest of the staff there. I'm glad of the warm welcome they have given this series.

# 1

"Remind me again why I said I'd do this?" I whispered to Lisbeth, who knew me better than almost anyone in the world, except maybe my parents. I kept my voice down because we were waiting in the wings of the high school's stage, watching the good citizens of Asheboro, Maryland, come in and find seats, so they could listen to me telling them how I thought we could transform the sleepy town into a place that tourists and historians would want to visit — and leave some of their cash behind. If that didn't work, the town would probably shrivel up and blow away, and I'd get the blame.

"Because you're the best person for the job," Lisbeth whispered. I knew she had my back, because she was the one who had called me and begged me to come help the town, and I'd been foolish enough to say yes. She was also standing behind me so that I couldn't turn and run away.

"You know I hate talking to crowds of people," I whined. She'd seen me botch my one stab at taking part in our high school debate team, in this same auditorium. Come to think of it, that was the last time I'd spoken to more than a dozen people at one time. I'd forgotten how terrifying it could be.

I checked my watch: ten of eight. Still time for even more people to drift in, ready to throw rotten tomatoes at me. This year there was a bumper crop of ripe tomatoes.

This was a special event for Asheboro, maybe even unique. While town meetings happened occasionally, seldom in my memory had there been one that affected the future of the town and all its residents. It sounded melodramatic to put it that way, but unfortunately it was true: if I couldn't help the townspeople find a new source of revenues for this struggling town, it was doomed. I knew I couldn't use dramatic words like *doomed* because people probably wouldn't believe me, but somehow I had to get them to believe that things in Asheboro really were that serious. If I could.

Over the last month or so I'd come up with a general proposal, but there were still a lot of holes in it, the largest ones in the budget. I could probably spin a good story about what could be done to transform the place, but I couldn't begin to tell them how to pay for it. The fact that a major storm had swept through recently and damaged a lot of the buildings along the main street, and then the bank manager had embezzled most of what little cash the town still had, didn't make my job any easier.

Lisbeth tugged at my jacket. "You might as well get started. A lot of these people have kids at home and will want to get back. Just tell them the truth, and keep it simple. Now, go!" She gave me a gentle push toward the stage.

Since I couldn't recall ever attending a town meeting here, although in my own defense I'd left for college and never looked back, I had no idea what kind of reception to expect. Stony silence would not have been my first choice. But here I was, and I had to move forward.

"Thank you all for coming tonight. I know you've got busy lives, so I'll keep this short and to the point." I swallowed as many pairs of eyes stared blankly. "If you've lived here for any length of time, you may remember me. I'm Kate Hamilton, and I grew up and went to high school here. Until about three years ago my parents lived in the same house they always had, before they moved to Florida." The crowd still looked like it were made up of zombies. "All right, how many people in this room have lived here for most of their lives?" A few hands went up. "Twenty years?" A couple of dozen hands. "Ten years?" About the same number — which was telling me something: nobody seemed to have any reason to move to Asheboro, and that had been true for a while.

"Let me be honest with you. When I finished high school, all I wanted was to get out of town." Several people laughed at that. "I went to college, and then I found jobs in other places. I never planned to come back, especially after my folks left. So why am I here now?" I waited for a response that never came.

I pushed on. "Because a very good friend of mine, who I've known since high school here — Lisbeth Scott — came to me to tell me that the town was broke and things weren't going to get any better unless something big happened. And she told me flat out that the town was desperate, and I was the only person she could think of who could help. And here I am."

Finally someone spoke. "Why'd she think that?" said a guy near the back of the room.

"You'll have to ask her that, because I'm

still wondering. Look, how many of you know what kind of shape this town is in?"

"Physically? Financially?" the same guy said.

"Physically, all you have to do is walk down the main street. It looks shabby, tired, like it got left behind while the world moved on."

"Why is that?" someone else asked.

"Please, don't throw things at me. I grew up here, so I can say what I see and what I believe. This is and always has been a good town, with good people living in it. But the only industry was the shovel factory, and that closed long before most of us were born, and nothing came along to replace it. We're too far from Baltimore to make it an easy commute. The train line passed us by a century ago. There was never any kind of important battle or big historical event here. It's pretty and peaceful and quiet, but you can't pay the bills or send your kids to college on that. So people have left, and nobody's replaced them. And Asheboro has just drifted along the way it always did, until very recently."

I scanned the crowd to see if I had their attention. At least no one had gone to sleep yet.

I went on, "And then the town council

found some gumption and decided to buy the Barton estate and make something out of it. Which took all the money you had. I applaud the courage and the hope it took to do that, but it's not enough to have a house, no matter how gorgeous, without any other reason to come to this town. So you people really have only one shot at thinking outside the box and saving the town."

"And that's where you came in?" a middle-aged woman closer to the front spoke. "Why are you qualified to do anything about this mess?"

I focused on her, because it was a valid question. "I don't claim to be an expert, in city planning or in finance. The biggest project I've ever managed was a Baltimore hotel, and one in Philadelphia before that. But nobody else seems to have stepped up, and all I've agreed to was to try to come up with a plan that might work. And in case you're worried, I'm not getting paid for this. I just don't want to see the town die."

"And you think you have some ideas to fix this?"

"Maybe. But it's going to take some cooperation from the people in this town, particularly those who have a business in the center of town."

"And money? Higher taxes?"

"I know there's no money, and how could anybody raise taxes here when salaries and revenues are in the tank? I may be inexperienced, but I'm not naïve. Just hear me out. You don't have to vote on it or support it in any other way, at least not yet. If you have any suggestions, I'd love to hear them. But let me say one thing: to make this work, you all have to commit to it and work together. If you can't do that, it's over."

I could see that the natives were getting restless. So much for the big buildup. Time to get my Big Idea out there and let it sink or swim.

"Settle down, people — I'm just getting to the good stuff. I propose that we turn the central blocks of Asheboro into a Victorian village, as authentic as we can make it. And an extension of that would be the Barton mansion outside of town. In case you don't remember your local history, Henry Barton was the owner of the factory on the edge of town, and easily the richest man, and his house, if you haven't seen it, is a magnificent example of high Victorian architecture *and* it's in good condition. It wouldn't take much work or money to make it shine. The challenge is to bring the rest of the town up to that standard."

"When you say make this place a Victorian

village" — the speaker made air quotes — "what the heck does that mean? Level it and rebuild the whole thing? With what money?"

"Have you taken a look at the buildings on Main Street?" I challenged him. "Since the storm? Well, I have. And what I discovered — and I'll admit it surprised me — is that most of the buildings that date back to 1900 or even before are still there under a century of siding. Believe it or not, the village is still there. Now, many of you who kept your insurance paid up will probably get a small settlement for damages from the storm. If you were going to repair your shops, you'd have to peel off the newer stuff anyway, so you can put that money toward repairing what's underneath. Maybe replace some windows with older models, and patch up the roof. Then you gut the interior and rebuild it to look the way it would have been in 1900, which would probably be cheaper than going modern with it."

"What about stuff like lighting and plumbing?"

"As long as what you see looks authentic, what's behind the walls and under the floors can be up to the minute — and probably would have to be to meet local building codes."

"And why on earth would anybody come

to this town to look at all this stuff?" demanded another man.

"Because up front we decide to make it as authentic as possible, so visitors can believe they really have stepped back in time. It's a small town. It wouldn't take much to fix enough buildings so that all anyone standing in the center of town would see is only what would have been there in 1900. All the modern stuff like gas stations and supermarkets and fast-food joints are already outside of that, so normal life could go on. Have any of you been to Sturbridge Village in Massachusetts, or Monticello, or Williamsburg? That's the look I'm aiming for. It would feel *real.* And this place is close enough to the major battle sites in this state, or even in Pennsylvania, that it wouldn't be much of a detour for people, if we promoted it right. Okay, that's the basic outline. What do you think?"

One woman who I recognized from the town council said thoughtfully, "I'd like to see some more detailed cost analyses for this. And what about people who hate the idea? It sounds like everybody would have to be on board to make it work — you couldn't have a Starbucks on Main Street because then you'd lose the illusion."

"You're absolutely right. That's why we'd

need some true cooperation to make this work. But let's think optimistically. If you gag at the idea of running a candy emporium or a corset shop on Main Street, it's altogether possible that someone else might want to, and would buy you out at a fair market rate." I took a deep breath. "Let me tell you, nothing has to be decided tonight. I want you all to go home and think about the idea, and then we can meet again and you can say what you think. You love it, or you hate it — you have a right to your opinion. Talk it over among yourselves. Take the time to walk around town and really *look* at it — at the way it is now, and at the way it could be. But if you want to go on living here, raising your children here, retiring here, something has to be done. Thank you for listening."

I turned and walked offstage, mainly because I was exhausted, and I wasn't prepared to answer any questions because I'd told the crowd pretty much everything there was to this very preliminary plan. If enough people hated it, I'd go back to my prior life and look for a new job. But so far I'd had a lot of fun imagining the possibilities.

Lisbeth stopped me with a hug before I could escape. "You were terrific! I think they got the general idea without being swamped with details. Are you going to be able to meet with them in smaller groups if they have questions, which I'm sure they will?"

"I hope so, although I haven't made any plans for that."

"You're still staying at the B&B?"

"For now, at least. Ryan's okay with it, and the dining room would work well enough for small group meetings. You think they'll go for it?"

"Based on the expressions I saw from people in the crowd, I'd say maybe. I think you had them interested by the end there, but not committed."

"It's a lot to take in all at once, I'll admit. But it's not like we have a deadline."

"You should set a deadline for a decision, though," Lisbeth said thoughtfully. "If you don't, they'll just keep bickering about bits and pieces and never decide anything."

"How long is long enough?" I asked.

"Are you still thinking about having some kind of opening event by fall?"

"Maybe. I won't know if that's even possible until we take a hard look at what kind of shape the buildings are in. And you do know that we don't have any money — cash or credit — so we'd have to get started on the fundraising side of things ASAP."

"True. So set a date two to three weeks out and demand an answer. I know it seems short, but you've got to start somewhere."

I could feel my eyelids drooping as my adrenaline crashed. "Let's get together in the morning. Maybe things will look different then."

"My place? I'll give you breakfast and tell the munchkins to keep the noise down to a dull roar."

"Great. But not before eight o'clock."

"Deal. I'd better head home myself now. See you in the morning."

The crowd had dispersed quickly. I made my way to my car in the parking lot and drove the few blocks to the bed-and-breakfast that had previously belonged to my former high school nemesis, Cordelia Walker, now deceased and not widely mourned. Her ex-husband, Ryan Hoffman, owned the building now, but was in no hurry to unload it — he was one of the first to hear my vague plans and he seemed enthusiastic. The fact that he was a corporate attorney was icing on the cake.

I parked alongside the building and let myself in, managing to figure out the alarm system without setting it off. I shut off the outside light and turned to find a man standing a few feet away, grinning at me.

"Lady, I'd buy anything you're selling," he said.

"Josh, if I weren't so tired you would have terrified me. I didn't see you in the auditorium."

"Traffic was jammed up outside of Baltimore, but I wouldn't have missed it. I was in the back."

I wasn't sure why Josh was so invested in this off-the-wall idea of mine. Or maybe it was me he was interested in? We'd been involved for like fifteen minutes, but stranger things had happened. I decided to ask a safe question. "Do you think the good townspeople will go for the idea?"

"I'll give it even odds, but you did a good job. We'll just have to wait and see."

We? "Tomorrow. I'm exhausted. Oh, Lisbeth asked me if I wanted to meet for breakfast at her place. You want to come with, or would you rather head back to the city?" There: I'd laid it on the table. Did he want to go public with our whatever it was, at least to my best friend?

"Actually, I'd like to see what kind of feedback she's heard, after round one. I can go back to Baltimore after breakfast."

"I told her eight o'clock, so there's no rush in the morning."

"I'm happy to hear that. Uh, does she

know about us?"

"That we are an 'us'? Maybe. We haven't talked about it, but she's pretty perceptive. Does that bother you?"

"Not at all."

# 2

I'd be the first to admit that this was not the ideal time to start a new relationship. I was still smarting from having lost a job that I loved, through no fault of my own. When Lisbeth had contacted me, I had jumped at the chance to get out of Baltimore, hoping to clear my head and gain some perspective on what to do next. Instead I'd found myself sort of committed to overhauling the whole infrastructure of the town where I'd grown up, when I wasn't even sure it was possible. And the fly in the ointment was finding my high school tormenter, Cordelia Walker, town council member, half-hearted bed-and-breakfast owner, and bona fide bitch, dead on the steps of the Barton mansion, the single most important keystone for my grand renovation project. So of course I had to get involved in solving the murder, if I wanted any part of my plan to move forward. The fact that Cordy had been married to my high school sweetheart paled in the face of all the rest.

Then there was Josh. Joshua Wainwright, respected professor at Johns Hopkins in Baltimore, a major university; expert in nineteenth-century industrialization in the mid-Atlantic states, which could come in very handy in Asheboro; recently divorced (hmm, was that an important consideration at the moment?); and someone who could handle himself well in a crisis. We'd gotten kind of close in the short time we'd spent together solving Cordy's murder, but I had no idea about what his long-term plan was. We'd scored an academic coup when we'd found significant historical documents in the attic of the Barton house, but would he just write up a scholarly article and disappear back to his life in Baltimore? Or was he hoping to find more lost treasures in this sleepy town?

But he was willing to brave breakfast with Lisbeth, and I'd give him points for that.

We'd taken separate cars to Lisbeth's house, and he was following me. When we'd parked in her driveway, we stopped for a moment to confer before going inside. "What's the game plan?" he asked.

"As you suggested, I want to get Lisbeth's read on the crowd. She's lived here all her life, grown up with these people. Much as I hate to admit it, it's possible that the citizens, particularly the shopkeepers on Main Street, have lost hope and are already looking for an escape route. They may not want to invest their time and efforts in beating a dead horse."

"Lovely metaphor," Josh commented.

"I didn't say I believed that, but I accept the possibility. And even if people are behind the idea, as long as it doesn't cost them much, it may not be possible. I've made some pretty big assumptions about whether the buildings are structurally sound and how much money we'd need to scrape together to make this happen. And then there are time constraints. I started out thinking, *Oh, no problem, we can get the work done over the summer and be ready for a grand opening in the fall.* But I may have been a bit overoptimistic."

Josh grinned. "You think?"

"Hey, I'm trying to sell the idea. I have to look enthusiastic, don't I?"

"It helps," he agreed. "Have you given any thought to what you're going to do if the insurance money and sweat equity aren't enough?"

I sighed. "I'll just have to find other sources. I do have contacts in Baltimore, who I've worked with in the past. And I even have friends in Philadelphia. It's just a matter of how I pitch it. Maybe you could tap some of your collegiate buddies and present this as a good research project for urban planning majors."

"It's a nice thought — let's file that for later."

"Josh, I think we're getting ahead of ourselves. First we need a plan. Can we just go in and talk to Lisbeth while her impressions are still fresh?"

"Lead the way."

When we approached the door we ran into Lisbeth's husband, Phil, and their two kids, Jeffrey and Melissa. "Hi, Kate, sorry but we're running late, Lisbeth's waiting for you, see you later, come on, kids," he said, heading for the family van.

"Remember to breathe sometime, Phil," I called to his retreating back. He raised a hand but kept moving.

When I turned back, Lisbeth was standing in the doorway. "Kate, come on in. Hey, Josh — I didn't know you'd be joining us," Lisbeth said with an evil gleam in her eye.

"I asked him to — he's got a great background in nineteenth-century history. And you can draw any conclusions you want about the fact that he's here at eight o'clock in the morning."

"Oh, I did that a while ago. So, is this going to be a short meeting or a long one?"

"Well, Josh needs to get back to Baltimore, but I've got plenty of time. If you recall from last night, I said I'd give the townspeople time to think about what I said. How long is long enough, do you think?"

We followed Lisbeth to the kitchen, where there was coffee waiting. "I wouldn't wait too long. The kids will be out of school soon, and people kind of get distracted. You've got to feed them small doses of information to keep them thinking about it. So, what've you got?"

"Can we please eat? And the short answer is, not much — yet. I'll start with the big question first: Do you think this will work? Will people sign on for it?"

Lisbeth dished up bacon and eggs, and added some muffins to the plate. "I'd say maybe. Depends on how much work it is, and how much it will cost people out of pocket."

"Everybody knows about what Arthur did?" I asked. Arthur had been the longtime president of the only bank in Asheboro, until it was discovered that he'd been "borrowing" funds from the bank.

"You mean, blowing most of the Barton

money? Yes. So they know there's no help there."

"Tell me this: What percentage of the movers and shakers of Asheboro were there last night?"

"If you count the people they'll share the information with, maybe thirty percent. On the plus side, a lot of them are the ones who have the shops in town."

"Did they look happy? Or at least interested?" I asked hopefully.

"Maybe," Lisbeth said, although she didn't sound convinced. "Look, nobody is going to get excited until they know what it costs."

"If I may interrupt," Josh said, "I think you're thinking in Baltimore terms, Kate. Things move faster in a city. Asheboro is pretty rural. You have to give people time to digest this. Do *you* have a deadline of your own?"

I looked at the two people sitting across from me at the kitchen table. They were both staring at me with oddly similar expressions, which included some element of concern — or was that pity? I had to make an internal effort to step back and take a look at how I was behaving. Why was I in such a rush? I had no idea how long Asheboro's money would last, or what would happen if they didn't pay their bills. Would the lights go out? Would the water stop running? Would all the people in town pick up and walk away like a pack of lemmings?

Or was it that I had no job and no plan for my own future and I was desperate to find something to distract myself?

I took a deep breath and laid my hands flat on the table. "I'm sorry. You're right, Josh — I'm pushing too hard. I didn't even know about this mess until a month or two ago, and I have no reason to believe that it's at a crisis point now." I turned to Lisbeth. "You came to me because you believed I could help Asheboro. But I need to listen to you, because I haven't lived here for years, and even I can see that things have changed since I left. You can tell me who I need to convince, and what it will take to do that. I have to be willing to admit that I am so far out of my comfort zone!"

Next I turned to Josh. "Josh, you're at the other end of the spectrum. You're a complete outsider, but you bring some special skills to the table, and we need those. I think we could make a good team, if you're willing to take the time from your day job. I accept that this crazy scheme simply may not work, but at least we will have tried. And I appreciate your telling me that I'm charging into the middle of this like a mad cow. So, what do we need to do first? Apart from letting people have some time to think things over?"

Lisbeth looked tentatively at Josh, then turned back to me. "First you need to collect some basic information, like who owns which shop. How long have they owned it — which is to say, how deeply are they committed to it? Are they getting old? Thinking about retiring? And then there's the flip side of it: What shops do you want to see, assuming you have four Main Street blocks to work with? What about the side streets? And if you have certain kinds of shops, what supplies are they going to need, and should they be close by or can they be outside of town? Like, for instance, a stable that rents out carriages, or a driver and carriage together. Think early taxis. That means you have the carriages themselves, and they'll need maintenance. And you'd need horses, which need to be fed and kept clean, and their poop has to be cleared out. Tackle. And feed — how much, and what kind of storage would that take? Near or far? And that's just the one business. Sure, not every shop is going to take that kind of outfitting, but I'm guessing a good number will."

I grinned at her. "Lisbeth, you've been

thinking about this, haven't you?"

"Well, yes," she admitted. "It helps me go to sleep at night."

"There are other things you have to think about too, you know," Josh said. "Police — they'll need a station of some sort, even if it isn't big. A firehouse. Even in 1890 they had pumper trucks, only they were horse-drawn. Which would mean the same problem with housing and feeding the horses. I assume there's a church?" When Lisbeth nodded, he went on, "I hope it at least looks like it's from the same era?"

"It does," she said. "There are a couple of newer churches, but they were built outside the downtown. What about food? You'd probably have a greengrocer in town, maybe a butcher shop. A lot of country people kept chickens themselves," Lisbeth pointed out.

I jumped in. "Is there a printer in town, or close by? We need some promotional materials for all this."

Lisbeth nodded. "We can find one, I'm sure."

I was beginning to get into this. "Is the old newspaper still in business?"

"Yes, only it's a weekly now."

"How about a hotel? Not a really big one, but bigger than a bed-and-breakfast, and more central. Maybe with a tearoom?"

Lisbeth looked briefly perplexed, and then her expression brightened. "The Emporium! You remember that, don't you, Kate? Or maybe you never paid much attention to it. It started out as a small hotel, but people kind of stopped coming, so it was converted to what I guess you'd call an early shopping center. They took out a lot of the internal partitions, shored it up, and installed a bunch a small stores. We'd have to check with an engineer, but I bet it could be unconverted or whatever you want to call it."

"How many rooms?" I demanded.

"Hey, it was before my time. But I'd guess fifteen, maybe. It was enough for the people passing through. And it did have a tearoom on the ground floor, although the kitchen's long gone."

I was getting itchy again, now that the ideas were blossoming. "You have a fair-sized whiteboard or corkboard somewhere here?"

"Sure — the kids use them a lot. Why?"

"I need to see this laid out so I can visualize it," I said impatiently.

Josh interrupted, "You're getting ahead of yourself, Kate. There are some basic questions you need to address. Say you do get this up and running within a year. How many people do you hope to attract? Will you have enough housing for them? Or do you send them to the chain motel on the outskirts? Would that spoil the illusion? And so far there's only one place to eat in town, in your grand scheme. Again, how many people will you be able to feed? And where will visitors park?"

*Way to pop my balloon, Josh.* "You raise some valid points, Josh, but there are some things I do have experience with. One of them is advertising to a target audience. We would have to ensure that everything is first-rate, not just thrown together, and then we pitch it at committed historians, historical societies, Civil War re-enactors, and other people like that. A true Victorian experience, but not cheesy. And we price it appropriately. That's how you manage that kind of situation."

"Point taken," Josh said. "So now what?"

"Okay, then. First we put together what shops we want, that belong in a middle-class small town in the country. Then we look at which shops have survived and see if there's some overlap with what we think we want now. Then we talk to the people who own and manage those shops, to see if they're interested, or if they'd want to take part in this at all. If not, we figure out how to find people who would welcome a chance to rebuild part of the past and how we could attract them."

"You forgot the big step, Kate," Lisbeth said. "Find money."

"No, I just think these things need to be done first. If nobody wants renewed old stores, it's moot. But you're right: we need to find the money to pay for it. I don't think local contributions will be enough. Josh, I'm sure you know some people in the historic community in Baltimore. Maybe they won't want to give, but they may sit on boards or belong to organizations that have funds. And I've got a friend in Philadelphia who's spent half her adult life in fundraising. She's already seen this town and gotten my thumbnail sketch, and I think she'd like to help."

"So there you go," Lisbeth said, smiling. "You've just planned the whole thing. Piece of cake!"

I certainly hoped so.

# 3

"Sounds great," Josh said. "But you've ignored the elephant in the room."

I looked blankly at him, and then I realized what he meant. "The factory."

"Exactly."

"You know, I'm so used to seeing it there, I don't even think about it. It's like part of the landscape. What are you thinking?"

"Does it stay or go?" Josh asked.

I glanced at Lisbeth. "What kind of condition is it in?"

Lisbeth shrugged. "As far as I know, it's not as bad as it might be, even though it's stood empty all these years. Still, it would probably take even more work and money than all the Main Street shops together to fix it up. What would you want to do with it?"

I was torn. It was a big hulking building, yet it solidly anchored one end of the town. It was built as a factory and it looked it —

multistory, lots of brick, with small high windows and not much charm. All the exterior decoration in the world wouldn't make it beautiful. But I seemed to recall Josh mentioning once that it had a significant connection to the history of Asheboro, and we should certainly investigate that before we decided anything. And taking it down and carting away all the rubble would make the downtown a dusty mess for some significant amount of time.

"I don't suppose we could attract a new manufacturing tenant?" I suggested.

"Probably it would be hell to bring it up to code for manufacturing anything," Josh said.

"Art gallery? Performance center? Some combination of the two? Or maybe a conference venue?" I tossed out. None of those felt right to me.

"You'd have to take a look at the inside to see what the spaces are like. And there would be a parking problem if you're thinking of crowds," Josh pointed out.

"Anybody know any museum collectors who are looking for display space?" I asked hopefully, to be met with silence. "Or serious collectors of Civil War memorabilia? There should be plenty around. Maybe we could make it a cannon museum."

"Cannons? Seriously, Kate? Why don't we shelve that particular building for now?" Lisbeth said. "If you don't get the other, easier parts filled in, you won't have to worry about it."

"True," I admitted.

"Yeah, yeah," Josh muttered. "Any plans for a new librarian, Lisbeth?"

"It hasn't been all that long, Josh," Lisbeth protested. "And everyone was so used to seeing Audrey behind the desk there that they can't imagine anyone else. Plus the town council has been so discombobulated that they haven't had time to think about it."

"I know it's not urgent," Josh said, "but I was wondering how much town history and genealogy is squirreled away at the library. That's something else that could be worked into the former factory, made more accessible."

Maybe we were grasping at straws. "You know, there's no such thing as the universal factory. I don't have to tell you that, do I, Josh? The late nineteenth century was a time when things were really busting out all over. What we need is a hook here, something with some history relevant to the town, not just something we picked out on Wikipedia or threw together because it was easy. I hate to admit it, but I don't know enough about the history of the town to come up with any good ideas. You told me a while back that it was originally a shovel factory, right?"

"I did, and it was," Josh replied.

"Can you see making a showplace for shovels? I mean, I know they're kind of essential, but are they sexy?"

"I can't say that's a word I ever associated with shovels," Josh admitted, smiling. "But you're still getting ahead of yourself. Start making lists — that's what I do when I'm stuck. And start talking to people in town here — no pressure, just chatting. See if anybody remembers their fathers or even their mothers working at the factory back when it was still open." He glanced at his watch. "I'd really better hit the road now. Let me know when you come up with a next step, or you want something in the way of research from me. Walk me out, Kate?"

We both stood up. "Sure. Lisbeth, I'll be back in a few."

Lisbeth smiled. "Take all the time you want."

When we reached Josh's car I asked, "What's in this for you, Josh? You just like hanging out with me, or is there something more?"

"Spending time with you isn't enough?

But you're right. What you — *we* — have here is a town preserved in amber, where nothing has really changed in more than a century. You want to peel the plastic skin off it and reveal what's still underneath. That's a real find for a historian like me, and I want to do my own archeology here before other people get wind of it. As for us, well, there are a lot of doors to choose from, and we've got time to explore them."

"Pretty words, pal. But I've got plenty of things to work out for myself, so I guess that works for me too. Drive safe, will you?"

"Of course."

I turned away as he pulled out of Lisbeth's driveway, and I rejoined her in the kitchen.

"More coffee?" she asked.

"Sure. There's nowhere I have to be, and my head is spinning. You have any observations?"

Lisbeth refilled my coffee mug. "I like Josh."

"Let's not go there right now, okay? I want to wrap my head around this project. You do realize that it may never get off the ground?"

"Well, yes, but at least you can do your homework and talk to people before you give up."

"Who said I was giving up?" I protested.

"It's just that I have a lot to learn about Asheboro as it is now. I'm in an odd position: I remember what it was like when I was growing up, but obviously I see it differently now. How would you describe the overall mood of the town?"

Lisbeth thought for a moment. "Apathetic. Maybe depressed. The whole decline was kind of slow, even subtle. But there are no new jobs coming, so no new people, no new investors. People who live here like the place and their neighbors, but they've still got to pay the bills, and those keep growing. Are you sorry I dragged you into this?"

"No. It's an interesting challenge, and it came at the right time, when I need something to distract me." I cocked my head and studied her. "Can I ask you something?"

"Sure," she said cautiously.

"Do you want to be part of this project? I mean officially, not just behind the scenes."

"You mean, like a job?"

"Sort of. Obviously there's no real position, and certainly no money at the moment, but I'm asking for a commitment of a certain amount of your time, to get this off the ground."

"Kate, I've got kids, and school's out very soon. Where am I supposed to find this time?"

"Do they go to day camp? Would their grandparents step up for a week or two and look after them? I know this sounds very selfish of me, but your being part of this could make a real difference. You'd be the insider — people know you and like you. Josh is clearly the outsider. Me, I fall somewhere in the middle."

"Kind of like the Three Musketeers?" Lisbeth said, smiling. "Let me think about it, okay? You need to test the waters first anyway."

"You mean, talk to the shopkeepers. I know. Is there a chamber of commerce here? I need some current lists."

"Sure, not that it's very active. But I can put you in touch with the current head."

"See? You're being useful already." I stood up. "I'll get out of your hair now — I'm sure you have plans for the day. But thank you for letting us use your kitchen. After we're wildly successful, you can put up a plaque, saying something like, 'On this site Asheboro was reborn.' "

"Let's not order it just yet. Call me if you have any more questions, and I'll let you know if I think of anything. Oh, will Ryan be involved?"

"I haven't talked to him about any of this, except in very general terms. Tell me, do you think his legal expertise would be a good fit?"

"I think so," Lisbeth said after a few seconds of hesitation. "People around here still know him, even though his offices are somewhere else. Of course, he still owns property, as you know. So he's got a foot in each puddle, you might say — local connections, but broader skills. You going to ask him?"

"I haven't really thought about it, but we will need some kind of a legal structure to do this. Maybe even a nonprofit corporation or trust or something. Maybe I can pick his brain and then decide."

"You don't have any plans to see him soon?" Lisbeth said mischievously.

"What, you think I'm some sort of femme fatale, working my wiles on all the unmarried men around?"

"Just wondering. Is he charging you for using Cordy's B&B?"

"We haven't discussed it," I told her.

"Well, if this project happens, you might have to consider that as an in-kind contribution. Keep good records, will you?"

"Yes, ma'am, will do. But for now I need to go find a list of businesses in town. I'll report back when I know anything useful."

We made our good-byes, and I drove the

couple of miles back to the B&B, closer to the center of town. It would be a real plus to have Lisbeth in the mix for this, although she had a valid point about having to think about her kids. That was one issue I'd never faced. But surely they didn't spend every summer day sitting around the house and complaining they had nothing to do?

Three minutes later I pulled up in front of the B&B. Although Cordelia Walker's name didn't appear anywhere on the building, for me her ghost still lingered. How long would I feel like that? At least the bedroom she had used had been cleared of all her personal possessions, and I had no intention of using that room anyway. For the moment I had claimed the best room in the house, a spacious double in the front. Ryan, Cordy's ex and owner of the handsome building, was letting me use the place, but Lisbeth had made a good point. If we — whoever *we* ended up to be — were trying to raise funds for some serious remodeling, we needed to show that we were a professional organization, not just a bunch of kids — ha! — saying to each other, "I know — let's put on a play!" And that meant keeping track of expenses, and funding sources I'd approached, and contractors with whom we'd spoken or negotiated. I wondered briefly if any of the Baltimore firms I'd worked with would be interested in this much smaller project. I could make the argument that what it lacked in size, it made up for in prestige, which would be good advertising for them. But they weren't going to work pro bono, so somebody was going to have to pay for it.

I realized that Ryan's car was parked in front of the building. Did I want to speak with him today? I thought I'd better, because no doubt we were going to have to get lawyers involved sooner rather than later, and he was a local lawyer. If he turned down my sort of vague request, maybe he could suggest someone else who'd like to take it on. Nothing ventured, nothing gained.

I climbed out of my car and headed for the front door, which wasn't locked. "Hello?" I called out when I got inside. "Ryan? Are you here?"

"Upstairs," his voice drifted down. "Be down in a minute."

While I waited for him, I contemplated my choices. The layout of the house was typical for a high-end Victorian residence of its day, with a dining room and kitchen on one side of a broad central hallway, and a parlor and so-called library on the other.

Cordy had used the library as an office, not that she'd done much business. Did I want to take that over for the Asheboro Revitalization Project? At least it could be closed off; if I opted to use the massive dining room table, it would always look messy, which was not a good signal to any professional I wanted to talk to. Library it was, then.

No sign of Ryan yet. What could he be doing up there? I went down the hall and opened the door to the library and looked around. The dusty velvet draperies would have to go — they made the room far too dark — but the lace under-curtains would provide a degree of privacy. Cordy had kept a computer in the room, so the wiring worked, but a few more lamps wouldn't hurt. Maybe I should troll through the rooms upstairs and see if there were any other articles of furniture that could be useful. But I didn't expect to find a filing cabinet, which would look very out of place in the room anyway.

I could hear Ryan clomping down the uncarpeted stairs. "Kate?" he called out.

"In the library," I called back. He appeared seconds later. "Aren't you supposed to be at work?"

"This *is* work," he replied. "I own this

place, and I have to decide what to do with it now."

"Can it wait until we save Asheboro?"

He looked confused. "What do you mean?"

"Sit down and I'll tell you."

# 4

Ryan started talking as soon as he was settled in a chair. "I hear there was a town meeting last night."

I'd left a message with his secretary, but he hadn't bothered to attend. "Yes, there was. I asked the town to call one officially so I could talk to as many people as possible about plans to save Asheboro."

"I thought you'd given up on that."

Just because his ex-wife had died and I'd briefly been a suspect? I thought I might have redeemed myself by pointing to the killer. "No, I just got sidetracked by some other things. Like a crime. It was important to get that resolved before things went forward."

"What things?"

Was he deliberately playing dumb? "Will you promise to listen without interrupting? You'll have your turn."

"I'm all ears." He shifted in the chair in

front of the desk, while I assumed the power seat behind the mass of polished mahogany.

I went through the same spiel that Josh and I had given Lisbeth, polishing up some of the rough spots as I went. It took about ten minutes. Then I sat back in my throne and asked, "What do you think?"

"Is this plan for Asheboro hypothetical, or are you really thinking of going ahead with it?"

"Door number two. That's what yesterday's meeting was about. It was the first time that many of the merchants in Asheboro had heard about it, but their participation is going to be critical if this is going to work."

"Why on God's green earth do you think it's even possible?"

"Ryan, have you looked at Asheboro? I mean, really looked? I know you grew up here, but I doubt you paid much attention to the architectural details back then. Yes, it's shabby and run-down. But if you look past that, I think you'll find that most of the buildings on Main Street are structurally sound. It would take some investment to fix them up, but not a huge amount of money."

"What about the factory building?"

Funny that he'd zeroed in on that first. "We haven't come up with any firm ideas for that, but I believe we have to win over the Main Street merchants before we can tackle that."

"And the Barton mansion?"

"That's part of the bigger picture. You know that's in pretty good shape, both inside and out. It's not exactly in walking distance, but we can figure out transport easily enough." I hoped. "You have to admit it's a gorgeous building, and untouched in more than a century. And it ties in to the factory. I'm not looking for a Disney-type theme park. I want to create something authentic that takes you as a visitor back to an earlier, simpler time. Any real work would be to preserve or re-create the details — like what's on the shelves in the pharmacy — rather than starting from the ground up. Do you see what I'm saying?"

"I think so. Who's going to be on your team, if I may ask?"

"Me as overall coordinator. Josh as historical consultant. Lisbeth as community liaison." I thought she'd like that title — it sounded important. "Obviously we'd need a few more staff members, like an accountant. And in effect we'd all be fundraisers — we hit up anyone we're talking to. No contribution too small. And . . ."

Ryan raised one eyebrow. "Yes?"

"We're going to need legal help, in terms of deeds and titles, and establishing non-profit status for contributions, if that's appropriate. Are you interested?"

Ryan didn't answer immediately, and I wondered how I felt about that. Once we'd been a couple, sort of, and then Cordy had blown that out of the water. Then he'd been Cordy's husband, but that hadn't lasted. Lisbeth had been witness to both events. Now I was maybe involved with Josh. And Ryan no longer lived in Asheboro, so maybe he'd cut his ties much the same way I had cut mine. But did I really want him on our team? Or would that just create complications? Heck, I didn't even know if he was a good lawyer, or if his areas of expertise would even be useful to us.

"Can I sleep on it?" His voice broke into my reverie.

"Sure," I said glibly. "Nothing's going to happen fast. I just tossed the idea out last night and told people to go home and think about it. I don't expect an answer from anyone right away. And I have to get to know these people all over again. They probably remember me as that mousy girl who never opened her mouth. If they remember me at all."

Ryan's mouth twitched. "I think you've

made a good start — whittle it down and call it your mission statement. But there are a lot more things you need to know. I would suggest looking at the documentation for the bigger efforts, like Old Sturbridge Village or Williamsburg."

"Williamsburg had Rockefeller money behind it, didn't it?" I demanded. "And it's a lot bigger than what we envision. Plus it's a different era now — people's expectations have changed. And Sturbridge Village is on a larger scale too, and it's more early nineteenth century. We're aiming for the birth of the industrial age — the moment before things took off."

Ryan didn't respond to that point. "Sure, Williamsburg is bigger, but the principles hold. And, if I recall correctly, they have a main street with shops. Maybe you should take a field trip."

"Ryan, why do you know so much about places like those?"

"Don't you remember? Our school took a field trip to Williamsburg. And Mount Vernon, I believe. I liked what I saw."

"Oh." I hadn't pegged Ryan as a history buff.

"And pay attention to the information on the foundation. The language may not fit what you want, but it's a good model. Of course, maybe you don't want to go in that direction. But if you do, you'll need long-term plans. Incorporation. A board."

I was getting depressed. On some level I knew about most of this, in theory, but the sheer mechanics of making it happen were boggling. I realized that I was far more excited about the physical renovations than about the legal structure, even though it was necessary. "Ryan, are you trying to tell me that I can't pull all this together?"

"No, not at all," he replied quickly. "I respect your abilities and your drive. I'm just warning you that it isn't simple. And it's going to require the participation of quite a few people."

"Duly noted." I sighed. "Then let's go straight to the bottom line. In your estimation, is this project feasible, if we can raise the money, and will it accomplish what we want?"

"Which is to provide ongoing financial support for the town? Make it an attractive place for people and other small businesses? Maybe. I won't say no, but it's not a sure thing."

"Ryan, if you don't want to be part of this, I understand. I'd appreciate it if you could point me toward a person or law firm that could help, if it comes to that. But you're under no obligation here."

"Hey, I didn't say no. All I want is to be sure you've done your homework and know what's involved before I commit to anything. Like I said, I admire the way you're approaching this, but you have to understand it's going to mean hard work. And you've still got to win over the merchants."

"Got it. And thanks for being honest with me." I stood up. "Right now I've got to dig into that homework you keep mentioning. Let me know if you have any other insights, now that you know what's going on."

Ryan had stood as well. "And that sounds like a brush-off. Keep in touch, Kate."

"I'll do that. Lock the door behind you, will you?"

I watched as he left, wondering how things actually stood between us now. We'd already established that there were no lingering sparks, all these years later. There was no reason why he should feel any loyalty to Asheboro or to me. If he decided to help us, he would be paid and he would be recognized for his efforts on behalf of the town. And that was that.

I was hungry, despite my larger-than-usual breakfast. And I knew there was little in the way of food in the fridge. Clearly I hadn't planned for an extended stay, but at the very least I should pick up enough to feed myself for the next few days. But first I needed to collect some reading materials: a phone book (did anybody still distribute those?), maybe a list of businesses from the local chamber of commerce, and some sort of listing of small-town shops circa 1900. A quick online scan convinced me that the Williamsburg shops were far too early for my needs. Sturbridge was more promising, with shops selling pottery and tinware, wooden toys and games, and fabrics.

The chamber of commerce listing wasn't terribly helpful. Among the listings there were churches (some still in place, I assumed); a pump service and an electrical service, neither of which would have been relevant in 1900; a janitorial service (ditto); and a pet service. The bank and the library I already knew about. The large supermarket lay outside the bounds of my plan, as did the town's only gas station. A dearth of choices. Maybe Josh knew someone who knew what I needed to look for. Or I could just stroll along Main Street looking for the faded ghosts of old signs on the walls.

Or maybe common sense would prevail: I'd already made my mental list. Grocer, butcher, feedstore, hardware and tools, hotel and tearoom. I might as well start talking to people — maybe they'd have a wish list for small stores.

But not today. I'd already accomplished a lot, and now I wanted to treat myself to a visit to the Barton mansion. The bank had given me an official set of keys, after I'd signed several documents acknowledging that I had them, so I could come and go as I wanted, and right now I needed a dose of inspiration. Luckily I had managed to purge the image of Cordelia's bleeding corpse from my memory. She was gone, and the place had never really belonged to her, in any sense of the word. It was mine, in spirit at least, and I wanted the world to share and admire it.

Josh was still nominally the caretaker, but I knew he'd gone to Baltimore to teach today, so I'd have the place to myself. What's more, I'd wheedled the bank to disburse enough funds to update the alarm system, so there shouldn't be any vandalism or surreptitious snooping going on these days. There was nothing of particular financial value in the house, merely the house itself — its spaces, its architectural details, its luscious wallpaper, and so on. There might be some additional interesting documents still lurking in the attic — we'd struck gold when correspondence between nurse

Clara Barton and her distant relative Henry Barton was found in the attic — but it would take an expert to identify those of any value to anyone other than a historian. Besides, there was little to be done about them, since there was no current librarian to accept and store such a trove. I wondered if someone would step up and volunteer to help. I could think of one person in Philadelphia who would know who to ask for that kind of help, and I made a mental note to call her in the morning.

I locked up the B&B carefully and drove toward the mansion. Every plant along the way was in full leaf and/or flower at the moment, and the landscape looked lush. I had to stop to unlock the front gate and temporarily disable the alarm, and after driving through I made sure to shut the gate behind me and turn the alarm back on. Then I drove slowly down the winding driveway. I loved the way the very large house was concealed from prying eyes until the last hill, which, when I reached the crest, revealed the house nestled in a shallow valley. The only owner, Henry Barton, had been dead for over a century, but his vision for his home had survived. I truly hoped I could find a new purpose worthy of it.

I pulled up in front of the entrance and

got out of the car. Its ticking as it cooled was the only sound, apart from birds and the gentle swoosh of the wind. I couldn't bring myself to sit on the front stoop, because that was where I'd found Cordy. But the view was equally lovely from the back, so I wandered slowly around the house, trying not to look for evidence of decay. The place had been built to last, and had been lovingly maintained, thanks to Henry's foresight. He and his wife had had no children to leave it to, so he had lavished all his accumulated wealth on the house and property — and in his will he had left funds to ensure their survival, at least until a new owner came along.

I had to wonder how he had accumulated so much money from making and selling shovels. Josh had once explained to me the outline of the growth of that business, but somehow it didn't seem adequate to yield enough to support such architectural splendor.

Was I missing something? Was Henry a large-scale bootlegger or smuggler? The location seemed unlikely for that, and there was no hint of any kind of illegal activity among the sparse published accounts of the man's life. He hadn't come from a wealthy family, nor had his wife. So far the trunks and crates in the attic hadn't yielded any clues about his personal life, but there were many still waiting to be explored. There were enough people in town who remembered the factory when it was operating, or their parents would have, and they would probably have mentioned something if there had been something fishy going on there. Old stories tended to linger in small towns.

I settled down comfortably on the lush grass and admired the view some more. I would likely have fallen asleep, except I heard the sound of a car approaching the house. I assumed it would be Josh, and I was too comfortable to move. As I had guessed, a couple of minutes later he came around the side of the house and dropped down next to me on the lawn.

"You're back early," I commented.

"It was only a ninety-minute class. I gave the students short research assignments to get them thinking. You look relaxed," he said.

"I made some progress this morning, so I decided to indulge myself with a visit to this place."

"Anything useful?"

"Mostly things I need to follow up on. I talked to Ryan for a bit, and he gave me some tips about nonprofit corporations and foundations. But he did not commit to helping us — yet."

"Did he tell you that you were crazy?"

"Not in so many words, but he's not convinced. Did you have a chance to eat?"

"Not since Lisbeth's breakfast. You thinking about dinner?"

"My stomach is, but there's next to no food at my place. I was going to go food shopping, but it hasn't happened yet. You?"

"I think I could scrounge up enough to keep us alive for another day."

"So we don't have to move. That's good." I reached over and pulled him closer, and before I stopped thinking coherently I realized that I could get used to living like this.

# 5

When I woke up the next morning I felt good. Maybe some aspects of my conversations the day before had been a bit discouraging, but it was early days yet, and I'd gathered some useful information. I wasn't ready to make anything resembling a pitch to potential vendors in town, much less donors — I had a lot of polishing to do.

Since it was a weekday, the town's shops shouldn't be too busy, and it would be a good opportunity to talk to some of the townspeople one-on-one. I had to admit up front that I've never been good about cajoling people into doing what I wanted them to, which was one reason why I had been a behind-the-scenes manager at the Oriole Suites Hotel, rather than someone who interacted with guests. I was much more interested in creating a plan and then providing instructions on how to make it become real. Design I could handle, but people? Not so much. And frankly, I wasn't really used to taking the lead on any project. I was a good lieutenant; give me an order or a batch of them and I would see that they were carried out. I'd done that plenty of times. But to have someone — or in this case, something like an entire town — hand the whole unwieldy mess to me and say, "Here, make this nice, and don't spend too much money"? I was left floundering. Which I couldn't let show or it would never happen.

If I recalled correctly, I'd asked for this.

Well, I'd barely scratched the surface. I needed to get out there and start talking to people.

Josh began to make snuffly waking-up noises, so I figured I'd use the shower first, then investigate breakfast options. By the time I'd accomplished step one, Josh was upright, more or less, and I took myself downstairs and started some coffee. After a few minutes I could hear the water running upstairs. Five minutes later he ambled into the kitchen.

"I think I forgot to mention that I'm expecting someone this morning," he said as he poured a cup of coffee. "I might have been a bit distracted last night."

"Anybody I know?" I asked, my mind still

on who I needed to talk to in town.

"I doubt it. She's someone I met at a couple of conferences on urban history, here and there. She said she's doing some research and she wanted to talk to me. Her name's Alison Delcamp."

"Then I probably don't know her, unless she's written a lot about Baltimore. Don't worry, I'll get out of your hair. I want to start doing more up-close and personal research about the town buildings and who's using them now, just to get some ideas."

"Sounds like a good idea. What's your time line?"

"Unfortunately unrealistic," I said ruefully. "You must know by now that I'd hoped originally to have at least a start by fall, but I guess I hadn't realized how much work would be involved. Not the least of which is convincing the shopkeepers in town that this is a good idea. And I still don't know where the money's going to come from."

"One step at a time. Did you have any other thoughts about what to do with the papers in the attic?"

"Now that the word about the Clara Barton papers is public, more or less, I think it's important to find out what's there and move them to a safer place. One with more room so they can be inventoried."

"What if it's all junk?" Josh asked, sitting down across from me.

"Then I'll know we don't have to worry about them. But I'm not making plans until I know what's up there."

"How are you going to go through them?"

"I'm not an academic, and I'd really rather have a professional look at them. You remember my museum friend in Philadelphia, Nell Pratt? I'm hoping she can find us an archivist for a bit. How long do you think it would take?"

"In the simplest case — if they can be divided between 'house' and 'garden' and 'horses,' maybe less than a week. It depends on what level of detail you're interested in. Like 'house repair' versus 'comparative costs of slate versus wood shingles.' Are you looking for something in particular?"

"Not yet, but I'm curious. I don't expect we'll get as lucky again, as we did with Clara's letters, but we might as well find out."

"The attic isn't a good place to work for any amount of time," Josh said dubiously. "I'd bet it's pretty hot in summer."

"All the more reason to get the papers out of the attic. I know, they've been there for a century, and maybe the damage is already done, although the Clara letters seemed to be in good shape. I was thinking maybe we could transfer them to the library for now, since it's currently closed to the public." And it could be locked. And there would be a lot of eyes on it, given its location in the middle of town. Okay, maybe I was being excessively cautious, but we had found some treasures that last time we'd looked, so it made sense to protect the documents. "And there'd be more room to spread them out all at once."

"How do you plan to get them to the library? Moving archival documents requires special handling. And money," Josh pointed out.

"Josh, are you for or against this idea?" I demanded.

"I think in principle it's a good idea, but I'd want to know who's doing it. Including the moving."

"Let me talk to my friend, and I'll get back to you. And now I'd better head back to my place so I can get something done. I'll let you know what I find out."

I gathered up my things and made my exit. When I reached the front gate, I got out to test it. The town had scraped up the money for a new electronic lock for the gate, but I realized that it would have made sense to have one that could be operated remotely, since the mansion was at least a half mile away. Anyone coming or going had to stop, punch in the code to open the gate, drive through, then stop again and close it. It was securer than handing out keys to it willy-nilly, but not by much. I made sure to lock it when I reached the other side.

I reached the B&B quickly, and went toward the library at the rear of the building. I paused in the doorway, looking at it as a potential work space assuming I was around long enough to need one. It was certainly large, but the lighting wasn't very strong, and there were few surfaces to put things on. Like stacks of paper, which accumulated in snowdrifts, or had in any project I'd been involved with before. I'd have to check the other rooms to see if there were any tables that would be suitable. Of course, that assumed that there wouldn't be any guests staying here, at least not formally. It was handy to have some spare beds for out-of-town visitors, but if I was asking them for help or for money, the rooms should meet hotel standards. And be clean. I was *not* about to volunteer to manage a bed-and-breakfast, even sporadically. I wondered where Cordy had left her list of house cleaners.

*Kate, you're stalling again!* Okay, at this moment I had one mission: find a temporary archivist and hope he or she could put together a crew of qualified movers. The first person that came to mind was Carroll Peterson, a graduate student at Penn who my Philadelphia friend Nell Pratt had put me together with. Nell was the president of the prestigious Society for the Preservation of Pennsylvania Antiquities, so her recommendation carried some substantial weight in the historical community. I didn't really need to talk with her, although I always enjoyed that, but I wanted to see if what I was considering was something that Carroll could or should handle, or if I should ask for another recommendation.

I hit speed dial on my phone, with Nell's direct number, and she answered quickly. "Kate, how are you? Or rather, where are you? In Asheboro?"

"Exactly. Monday night I told anyone in town who would listen what I hoped to do with their town. Now I'm avoiding talking to the shopkeepers here so I don't have to hear them tell me I'm crazy, so I called you."

"I'm flattered, I think. Is there something you want from me, or just a sympathetic ear?"

"Both, I guess. Last time I saw you, we talked about going through the rest of the Barton papers so at least we have an inventory of them. Since then the town librarian has been fired" — I didn't see any need to go into the details — "so I thought maybe we could put the documents in the town library, at least temporarily. What I need now is an archivist with some basic qualifications, for a short-term job. You'd probably have a better handle on how long this would take than I would. What do you think?"

"I can ask Carroll Peterson if she could spare the time, since she knows the situation. If not, there are a couple of other people I could talk to. Of course you want this done yesterday."

"Not only that, but I can't pay her, although I can give her a place to stay and feed her. You do fundraising, right? This project isn't going anywhere unless I can show potential donors a hook, something that will get their attention. We got lucky with Clara's letters, but I'd like to think there could be some other interesting bits and pieces in the collection. Or maybe just the collection as a whole, as a glimpse into an earlier way of life. Does that make sense?"

"As much as anything these days. Am I right in guessing that you have no money for the project?"

"Yup — the bank president cleaned out the Barton account, so we're starting from scratch."

"Ouch," Nell said. "One more slightly more serious question: Do you believe there's anything of value up there? I know finding Clara's letters was a gift from heaven, but how often does that happen?"

"I know. It seems unlikely and I'm not counting on finding gold twice, but I'd feel better if Henry Barton's papers were safe. It's not urgent, so no rush, but if Carroll or someone else is available I'd really appreciate it."

"That's what I do — network a lot. When do I get invited out there again?"

"You know you're welcome anytime, Nell. And if you have any brilliant ideas about what a small rural town in western Maryland looked like in 1900, I'd love to hear them. With pictures, preferably."

"How about a fire engine?"

"A what? Of course, a fire station. Where would I get an engine? Horse-drawn?"

"I might know someone . . . ," Nell said, with a hint of mischief in her voice.

"I *knew* you were the right person to talk

to! Thank you!"

We hung up quickly after that. I felt about 78 percent better than I had when I'd picked up the phone to call Nell. A fire engine! People would love that, if it was an original. Of course, if we were to actually use it, we'd need more horses. Well, duh — we'd need a stable full of horses, so we could transport people out to the mansion. And a fair-sized carriage house would take up another piece of Main Street, all for the good.

I love it when a plan comes together!

# 6

After grabbing a quick lunch from what scraps I could find in the refrigerator — *Kate, go to the market!* — I gathered up my courage and set off for the heart of town. On foot, so I could study the details. I took along a pad and pencils and pens and my camera and even a measuring tape. At the rate I was going I was going to have to get a notebook to keep all the facts straight. And a better camera, so I could record things, before and after.

The B&B was well located, a short block from the first storefronts in town, close enough to walk but not so close that it would be noisy or attract too many vehicles. Heaven forbid that anyone should poach the B&B's parking spaces! I paused on the fringe of town to study the layout. The basic form no doubt went back to the founding of the country: one main road, church, town hall, library. Houses had gradually appeared on either side of the road. As more people migrated to the area, more houses were required. Eventually there were enough people to warrant a commercial center, and that's about where things had stalled in the nineteenth century. Barton's factory had more or less blocked one end of development, but there hadn't been much reason to expand commercially in any other direction.

But that all came before the time I was interested in. Once there was an actual town, with a center, had there been a standard town plan a century or more ago? Or had common sense prevailed? Horses — for that hypothetical carriage house serving both carriages and the fire department — would generate odors, so it would seem logical to put that at one end or the other. The factory occupied the far end of town, so it would have had to be near where I now stood at the opposite end. Was there any sign of it now? How many horses would have been needed, and how much space would each horse take up? Would deliveries of hay and feed come in at the back? It occurred to me that I should take a look at the back side of the stores. It wouldn't be sensible to block the main street just to unload whatever passed for a truck in those days.

What else? Did butcher shops smell bad in the days before dependable refrigeration? What did the butchers do with their scraps? Trash barrels? But how often would they have been picked up? And by whom? And where did the trash (and garbage) go? Had there been a town dump somewhere? I was pretty sure I'd never seen one, but how many students did? Combustibles in the trash could have been burned, in those halcyon days before people obsessed about air pollution. But food products? Manure? And what about the delicately named "night soil"? When did working plumbing come along, and how far did it extend? What did people do with their chamber pots?

"Do you need some help?" a voice interrupted my increasingly repellent thoughts. "Oh, you're Kate, uh, Hamilton, aren't you? I was at the town meeting."

"Yes, I'm Kate. I'm glad you came to the meeting. What did you think?"

The woman, who looked to be approaching sixty, with no makeup and her hair graying naturally, sighed. "You made it sound really nice, but that's a long way from making it happen."

"I know. I won't pretend it isn't. What's

your name?"

"I'm Laura Weston. Born and raised here. Before you ask, no, I'm not old enough to remember horses in the streets, but there sure were a lot more people walking in those days. Only a couple of people in town had cars when I was a kid. Used to be a bus to Hagerstown, though. Mom took us there to get school clothes, once a year."

"You must have seen a lot of changes. Do you have a business here?"

"Nope, I farm, with my husband. His family's land. He's at the feedstore right now, ordering stuff. I came along for the ride."

"Where's the feedstore?"

"Where it's always been — down at the end of town, across from the factory."

"So you do remember some things! Can we sit down somewhere and talk?"

Laura checked her watch, a large man's watch with a scratched face. "Sure — Jake gets to talking with the guys at the store and loses track of time."

"Where can you get something to drink — coffee, soda — without getting into your car and driving five miles?"

"There's a place behind the hardware store."

I realized I remembered it. I wasn't one of

the cool kids who hung out after school, but every now and then my friends and I would check out the place to see what we were missing. "How come you remember who I am?"

"I was a teacher until we inherited the farm from Jake's dad. Never had you in a class, but teachers used to talk about students in the break room. You were one of the ones we thought would go somewhere. Were we right?"

"Kind of," I admitted with a smile. "I've been a lot of places since I graduated from high school."

"And here you are," Laura said. "You're gonna save the town for us, right?"

"Lisbeth Scott thinks I am, but she may be the only one. Let me ask you, do you think it's possible and that I can do it?"

"Maybe. If it were up to me, I'd give you the rope and let you hang yourself."

"If nobody steps up now, what do you think will happen here?"

"I think we'll get annexed by one town or another, after a few years of arguing, and then we won't exist anymore."

"Is that a bad thing?"

"Hard to say, to tell the truth. The world keeps changing around us. I hardly know how to turn on a computer, but plenty of people work on one around the clock, so they can live anywhere. Saves gas, doesn't it?"

"I hadn't looked at it that way. Maybe I've lived in cities for too long — I keep thinking that bigger is better."

"Yup," Laura said. "Bigger noise, bigger lights, bigger bills for just about everything."

"Except gas," I reminded her.

"Hey, how about that drink? Think you can find the place?"

"Yes, now that you've reminded me."

Laura let me lead the way down a narrow walkway between two buildings, opening on a small parking lot, half-filled on this quiet afternoon. The small place — luncheonette? soda shoppe? — was in the middle of the block to the right, and we found a table and sat, and ordered iced teas. And then Laura proceeded to unload just about every memory she had about the Asheboro she remembered. I listened, and hoped I could remember enough of what she said without taking notes. No, she hadn't been around for the Victorian era, but what she did remember was a small town where everyone knew each other to chat with, that was relatively clean, with low crime. Where nobody was worried about impressing their neighbors but instead helped each other when there were troubles. Where everybody went to the funeral if a neighbor or even a relative of a neighbor died, because it was how you showed respect.

I had to think back to my early days in Asheboro, because I'd made a point of forgetting them. Had things been like that when I was growing up? I'd been a typical self-centered student and teen, so I hadn't been paying attention to what the older generation was doing. I'd have to call Mom and Dad soon and ask what they remembered about the town. But as I listened to Laura, I was beginning to realize that the vision I had of the de-modernized Asheboro was based on appearances but somehow missed the spirit of the town. Sure, we could pretty up the façades and stick in gaslights, but what about the people? Was it possible to create or re-create that earlier, simpler time and make it feel real for people just passing through? How?

And what would the citizens of Main Street think about that? Were they going to have to smile and make nice to strangers who showed up for an afternoon and oohed and aahed over the cute, quaint reproductions? And buy some of each to take home to their friends and relatives back home, wherever that was? And the merchants would pocket their percentage and pay the rent and live to sell another day. Was that enough?

Eventually Laura drained her glass and said, "Jake'll be wondering if I've run off with the mailman, so I'd better go find him. It's been a treat to talk with you, Kate. You made me remember things I hadn't thought about in years."

"You've given me a lot to think about, Laura." Like that I should overhaul my sketchy plan, even if I didn't know how. "I appreciate your sharing with me."

"Have I changed your mind?" Laura asked, her eyes serious.

"Yes and no. You made me see that making the place look clean and pretty is the easy part, but making it feel real to visitors is going to be harder."

"Don't worry — you'll figure it out. You're one of the smart kids, remember?" She stood up. "I'm gonna guess we'll be talking again. Hey, while you're around, you ought to talk to Ted — he's the owner here. He's been running this place since it opened."

"I'll do that. Thanks, Laura."

Out on the street I tried to decide my next step. I'd set some things in motion by asking Nell to find someone to clear out the Barton attic. But I couldn't assume I'd find treasure up there. Probably there would be a whole lot of old invoices, and maybe some discarded china wrapped in old newspapers.

I was planning to go back and collect my car so I could go food shopping when my phone rang, and it turned out to be Carroll.

"Hey, Carroll. You talked with Nell already?"

"I did, and I'd love to help out. Philadelphia can get pretty hot in summer, and besides, I need to shift gears, try something different. You want to inventory the rest of the stuff in the mansion attic, right?"

"Yes, and move the documents to the library, where they'll be safer. It's closed to the public at the moment, so there's plenty of room to spread things out. No, we don't have to do the moving, but you get the idea."

"Sure, good idea. I can be there tomorrow and we can make a preliminary assessment of what's what and how much space you'd need at the library. After that I'll have a better idea about how long it will take to make a first pass at the records. Then we can decide if there's anything worth exploring further."

"Sounds good to me. You're welcome to stay at the B&B with me."

"Beats commuting. How about I aim to

meet you there about ten?"

"You know where to find the place?"

"If I don't, my GPS does."

"I'll see you then. Thanks, Carroll — and thank Nell too, when you see her."

"Will do. Bye for now!"

I did an imaginary fist pump: one thing accomplished. Of course, there was still a long list. I still needed to get food, especially if I was expecting company, but since now I knew when Carroll was arriving, I thought I should check out the library and find out what state Audrey had left it in. Which meant I needed a key. Which meant I should talk to Mayor Skip and see if he could lend me one. I walked over to the town hall, hoping to catch him in his office at mid-afternoon on a weekday, and it turned out he was there. I nodded to his assistant as I walked in, and she waved me through to Skip's smaller room. He bounced to his feet and offered his hand.

"Hey, Kate, good to see you again. I hope you don't have anything dire to tell me, like there's a fault line under the town and we're all about to fall in."

I laughed. "No, Skip, nothing like that."

"So, what can I do for you on this fine day?"

"I wanted to ask you about using the

library to sort through the rest of the documents from the Barton house attic. I've got a friend coming from Philadelphia who knows something about library cataloging, and she's happy to help out. And of course Josh Wainwright can help. Actually, though, I don't know how much there is in the way of documents belonging to Henry — could be a dozen linear feet, or could be a whole lot more. But we won't know until we dig into them."

Skip waved his hand. "No problem. I'm guessing you need the keys, so you can come and go?"

"Yes, exactly. And someone who can help us move all the stuff too, but carefully. We're talking about a lot of Asheboro history. It would be great if you could find some people for me."

Skip grinned. "Many hands make light work, right? And it's a smart idea to involve as many of the townspeople as you can."

He was right — it would give people some sense of ownership of the project, and maybe they'd find something that inspired them. "That would be terrific! I don't want to get people's hopes up, but I'm certainly looking forward to learning more about the history of the town. I'm sure you know that if you live in the midst of it, especially when you're young, you don't really see a place."

"I hear you!"

"So, how did you end up running for mayor?" I asked.

"I could say, 'Nobody else wanted the job,' but I like the town and I figured I could do some good. I do have a day job — school principal, you may recall — which pays the bills and is pretty flexible, and I don't think anyone would call me ambitious."

"So Asheboro isn't a stepping-stone to higher office?" I asked, smiling.

"Not hardly," he said, returning my smile.

We spent a pleasant half hour comparing notes about what we remembered about the town, who we'd known in the past, how we'd decided to stay or leave. It was nice, getting to know someone who you knew but didn't know: we shared memories, but as far as I could recall, we'd never actually met when we were growing up. Finally I said, "I should let you get back to work. Do you have the library keys?"

"Sure do." He started rummaging through his cluttered drawers.

"Great! Oh, and do you know if anyone else in town has keys?" It wouldn't hurt to check, even though I truly doubted that anyone would sneak in to rummage through Henry Barton's papers.

"Not that I know about. We took back Audrey's, of course, but nobody else has shown any interest. Oh, and Cordelia's and Arthur's — you've already got their keys to the mansion, right? There's nothing in the library building except a lot of books, a couple of donated computers, and the family history stuff in the back. Pretty typical of a small-town library, I'm guessing."

"You're probably right. I just wanted to be sure, in case we find an original copy of the Declaration of Independence or something like that."

"That might solve a lot of the town's problems, don't you think?"

"I bet it would," I agreed. "Is there anything like an alarm system?"

"I don't even remember. Like I said, there's nothing important in there, and I can't recall that anyone has ever tried to break in."

When he finally found the key rings he was looking for, he pried off one ring with several keys on it and handed it to me. "Front and back are the same key. There's one for that basement — there isn't any attic — but I can't tell you what's down there. Audrey took care of all that. And I don't think there's any off-site storage, because that would have shown up on the town budget, and we've been keeping an eagle eye on that for a while now."

"Thanks, Skip — I'll take good care of the keys, and I won't mess anything up. I may want to clear off one or two of the big reading tables, but I'll make a note about where things were."

"Happy hunting, Kate!" the mayor said cheerfully, and then he was pulled away by his assistant, and I went on my own way.

# 7

I was certainly going to get plenty of exercise if I kept walking from one end of town to the other. As I made my way the few blocks to the town library, I found myself wondering — not for the first time — what kind of a man Henry Barton had been. Based on what little I knew of him, I thought it was safe to say he hadn't come to Asheboro looking for fame and glory, or even recognition. He had kept reasonably good personal records, not that they revealed much. Maybe he had become bored with plain old shovels, useful though they were, and had pushed the manufacturing envelope. Maybe his wife had proved a disappointment, or she was chronically ill, or had a nervous breakdown, or a stroke and could no longer communicate, and he had needed a constructive outlet?

I was getting far beyond my evidence. What did I know? Henry fought in the Civil

War, came to Asheboro and bought a modest farmhouse, married a woman about whom I knew next to nothing, remodeled the house extensively (for himself or for his wife?), never had children, built and then expanded the shovel factory and diversified its products, saw his wife die, and died himself around 1910. And there was the sum and total of the facts I knew about Henry's life, apart from his fleeting connection to Clara Barton. It seemed that the town hadn't paid him any attention. Had it been his choice, to hide in his private valley? Had his name been plastered all over the factory building in its heyday? Or had it said only SHOVELS?

I was getting impatient to see what was in the papers he'd saved, because things didn't quite add up.

At the library I let myself in, locked the door behind me, and fumbled for the light switch. I was relieved when the lights came on — at least the town hadn't cut the power. I stood for a moment with my back against the door; the last time I'd been in the building, librarian Audrey had poured her heart out to me, and now she was in prison awaiting trial. But that was then and this was now, and I was on a mission.

I looked critically at the available tables

and the surrounding space. After Audrey's abrupt departure, nothing had been changed, but Audrey had been scrupulously tidy, so it wouldn't take much to clear working space. I couldn't begin to guess how much space the papers would occupy, laid out here, but there was no reason why we had to spread everything out all at once. And once again I was getting ahead of myself. I should probably wait until Carroll had done a preliminary sweep of the materials in the attic and decided what was the most critical to review. After all, she was the library professional, and I was just a nosy bystander. I had no idea how Josh felt about original documents, although my impression was that anyone with scholarly pretensions valued getting back to the original source, because so often details were later inserted or deleted or simply manufactured after the fact.

I wondered how long this first pass would take. If we found nothing worth pursuing further, so be it. It wouldn't really affect the town project. After all, the town had existed before Henry had settled here, and had survived a century after his death, so any personal details he might have left behind seemed unlikely to be critical to the story of the town.

I jumped when I heard an unexpected rapping at the door. I turned to see a youngish guy — midtwenties? — standing outside in the growing dusk. I was reluctant to open the door to a stranger, but it seemed rude to ignore him. I walked over to the door and opened it. "Can I help you?"

The young man smiled politely. "Is the library open?"

"I'm afraid not. The town is looking for a new librarian, but at the moment there are no employees."

"Could you let me in? Please?"

"I'm sorry, but I don't work here — I had to ask permission from the town to get in, so the town knows I'm here." Giving him that bit of information made me feel a little safer. "You could ask someone there tomorrow. Is there something particular you're looking for?"

"Mostly family history. You keep that kind of stuff here, right?"

"Yes, there's a room at the back devoted to local families." I waved vaguely toward the family history room. "Have you done much genealogy?"

"Not really. I'm just starting out, but my folks said that some of the family had come from around here. Do you live in town?"

"No, I'm just visiting. I don't really know

how much is in the collections here. And, as you may have already found out, this kind of research always takes longer than you think it will."

"It doesn't look like a very big building," he said wistfully. "And I can't take a lot of time off from my job, but I needed a break. Maybe I could come back tomorrow?"

"Why don't you talk with the people at the town hall tomorrow, so they know you're here? And they can let you in? There may be people around later in the day, but I'm sure the town doesn't want people just wandering through."

"I guess that makes sense. I'll try that. Thank you." He smiled, then turned away and started walking back toward the center of town.

Had I done the right thing? I didn't feel comfortable letting him in, and I didn't have the time to keep an eye on him, and I certainly didn't want to leave him alone in the building. Still, I'd grown up in this town. It was peaceful, quiet . . . boring. No crime, no gangs. But it wasn't up to me to decide if this pleasant young man could be trusted. Let the town staff make that choice.

I went back to the B&B, retrieved my car, then went in search of basic provisions. As I drove back from grocery shopping, I decided I should make a feeble stab at cleaning up for Carroll in the morning. I doubted I'd have time once Carroll arrived, and I didn't want to miss any discoveries at the mansion. Tomorrow was going to be a busy day.

Rounding the corner toward the B&B, laden with plenty of coffee and breakfast foods, I was surprised to see someone sitting on the front steps. It was only when I got closer that I recognized Josh. Why was he here?

He stood up quickly when he saw me coming. "You weren't here."

Huh? "Yes, I know I wasn't. I went over to the library to see if I needed to move things around so we could work, and then I went grocery shopping. Why are you here? I thought you were expecting a visitor."

"Alison arrived, and we talked for a while. She's got some interesting ideas, and she decided she wanted to pick my brain some more, so she's going to stick around. I said I'd ask you if she could stay here, but she said she didn't want to be a bother and would stay at the hotel. From the way she was dressed, I don't think she was the type to enjoy a quaint and cozy B&B."

"I'm not exactly offended, you know. This isn't my place and I'm not going to worry about it. So why are you here?"

"To see you?"

"Oh. That's nice of you. And you can help me make up a bed for Carroll, if I can find clean sheets. I promised Carroll that she could stay here too."

"Carroll?" he asked.

"Yes. I told you, I called my Philadelphia friend Nell, and she called Carroll, who's already seen some of the Barton papers, who jumped at the chance to sift through a hitherto unknown collection of correspondence. So she'll be here in the morning. And I got the keys to the library from Mayor Skip, so we'll have a larger and better lit place to work."

"You really have been busy."

"There's a lot I want to get done, and not much time to do it. I don't want to miss the opportunity to get started. I take it you're staying for supper? I know there's some of Cordy's wine left. If you're interested."

"Lead the way. By the way, I think Alison's from Delaware — maybe you know some of the same people. She definitely won't be around tonight."

"Then let's go in. I actually bought some food, so we won't starve." I unlocked the door, disarmed the alarm, and led Josh toward the kitchen. I decided to open the wine before I tried to patch together something resembling dinner. "I think the library will work fine for what Carroll needs to do. Audrey left it in good shape, thank goodness." I handed Josh a glass of a red wine whose name I had only read about. "But one odd thing: some youngish guy came by and wanted to come in to do some genealogy research. For some reason he thought the library would be open. I guess he must be from somewhere else — someplace with large libraries that keep long hours. I told him to check with the town hall and see if they'd let him use it. I know genealogists, even amateurs, can get kind of manic about finding what they're looking for."

"As are researchers. Say what you will about online databases, but there are still caches of original documents that may never reach the internet."

"Is that why you came here?" I asked.

"No, not really. I can go back to Baltimore if I need more material. But this short-term caretaker thing sounded like the perfect job, because nobody ever bothers me. I got a lot of work done. At least until things started happening."

Things like murder. "Did you tell anyone at your college department about what you were doing? It wasn't because some colleague was looking to steal whatever you were working on?" I wasn't sure if I was joking.

Josh smiled. "Industrial history isn't exactly exciting, you know. And I've already got tenure. So, no, my life was kind of messed up, and I wanted some peace and quiet. Time to think. Although I will say that finding Clara Barton's correspondence was exciting, and it's not even my area of expertise."

"Heck, even I was excited, and I'd barely heard of the woman. But finding things like personal letters makes the people and the time when they lived seem much more real." I peered one last time into the refrigerator, but nothing else had miraculously appeared. "I vote for bacon and eggs and toast, because all I bought was breakfast stuff. Unless you want to go out and eat somewhere?"

"Bacon and eggs sounds fine. As long as there's more of that wine."

After we'd finished our sketchy supper, I asked Josh, "Do we have a strategy for tomorrow? Carroll's going to meet me here, and I assume I'll be taking her out to the mansion and turning her loose in the attic. Are you getting together with Alison?"

"Maybe. If need be, we can work in the

carriage house and leave the mansion and the attic to you and Carroll."

"I think that will work. Mayor Skip said he could find us some people to move the Barton files, but I assume Carroll will need some time to sort through the stuff in the attic before we start moving things. I think we need to see what Carroll finds, and how she wants to deal with the papers. It's hard to guess what might be there. Maybe Henry simply saved everything that passed through his hands. Maybe it includes all his love letters from Mary, or letters from his brothers after the war."

"What would you really like to find?" Josh asked, draining his wineglass.

"Where his money came from," I said promptly. "This might be more your turf, but I've been wondering about it. Even if he started with a lowly shovel factory after the Civil War, there still would have been setup costs, materials to buy, and so on. Maybe he was a brilliant businessman, saw the future coming, and made the most of his opportunities. But if the mansion is any indication, he made a *lot* of money very quickly."

Josh smiled. "I agree. It all seems to revolve around the money, one way or another. But let's wait and see what Carroll comes up with. Let's not get ahead of ourselves." He stood up. "I should get going."

"You don't have to leave, you know," I said carefully.

"Good. Because I don't want to. But I promise I'll be out of your hair before your friend arrives."

"Sounds like a plan."

# 8

When I woke up the next morning, Josh was gone. As I lay in bed trying to sort out what to do next, I realized it was a good thing I wasn't working at an hourly rate. Or, actually, working for anyone at all. Or accountable to anyone except myself. I wondered how I would explain to the town that the first thing I was doing to rescue Asheboro was wading through an attic full of dusty old letters and files. I could point to what we'd already found — the Clara Barton correspondence — but that wasn't going to bring the town any money, because I wanted to use those as a collection to showcase one aspect of the Civil War, or the postbellum period. Actually, I had no idea what the letters were worth financially, but I was pretty sure it wouldn't be enough to bail out the downtown district.

Nor could I imagine any other letters or documents that would bring in substantial sums. Maybe if Abraham Lincoln had spent his weekends at the Barton mansion and wrote polite thank-you notes each time, duly signed, there might be a profit, but I wasn't going to count my chickens. So what was I hoping for? Or was I just stalling for time, hoping I'd be slammed with a brainstorm? It seemed to me the best I could hope for was that a collection of prestigious letters might attract a different group of visitors, and that couldn't hurt.

I hauled myself out of bed, showered, and wandered down the stairs in search of breakfast. Since I had no newspaper, I entertained myself with thinking of alternative funding sources. Maybe I should talk to someone at Old Sturbridge Village or *This Old House.* Had the latter ever refurbished an entire town? They might be interested. Or I could contact vendors of period materials, like wooden moldings or brass doorknobs. Or I could go hunting for a single very rich benefactor and figure out what in Asheboro could I put his or her name on to commemorate a generous monetary gift?

My reverie, which was growing increasingly absurd, was interrupted by a knocking at the door, and I checked the peephole (which I assumed Cordy had added to the

Victorian door) before opening the door to Carroll.

"I know, I'm early," she apologized breathlessly, "but there wasn't a whole lot of traffic going this direction. It's good to see you again, Kate, and I'm looking forward to digging into the documents." She grabbed me in a quick hug. She must *really* be excited by this project.

"Come on in, Carroll," I said when she let go. "You want some coffee?"

"Of course. And you can fill me in on the plan, whatever it is."

"Let's just say it's a work in progress," I told her as we walked to the kitchen. I started more coffee, and gave her a quick summary of the B&B — she was particularly intrigued by the hidden compartments where Cordy had stashed her wine, although I told her that there were no documents lurking in them, only expensive wine. "Cordelia was not exactly an intellectual, and you can see where her priorities lay," I explained, with just a hint of malice.

Once we were settled with coffee and muffins, Carroll asked, "So, what is it you want me to do?"

"My overarching goal is to save the town by taking it back to how it looked around 1900. My personal goal is to use the Henry

Barton mansion as the gem in the setting, so to speak. It actually hasn't been touched since he died in 1911, but it has been carefully maintained. But it's a few miles out of town, so there are certainly details to be worked out, like how to get back and forth. But I want to go through his attic full of documents to see both if there's anything of value, and to glean whatever information there is about how the house came into being, how it was used, why Henry, who began as a simple soldier, put so much into making it a mansion, and how he could afford to do it."

"I hear you," Carroll said. "You want to use the place as a key to getting to know Henry."

"Exactly. And by extension, his impact on the town. The Clara Barton letters you've seen date to before he started building — or expanding — his home, so all the changes came after he sorted out his inheritance. But they didn't end there, because we know he was still improving things twenty or thirty years later."

"You told me he owned a factory in town?" Carroll asked.

"Yes, and it was the only industry in the town. Apparently it did well — he appears to be have been a good businessman — but after he died things kind of went into decline, with the changes in technology, and the demise of the factory kind of took the town down with it."

"Is the factory building still standing?"

"Yes, in surprisingly good condition. Henry built things well."

"And nothing has been done with it?" Carroll sounded surprised.

"You mean, is it a mega-mall filled with junk? Nope. I think any industrial metal items that could be recycled were removed a long time ago, but otherwise it's been empty for as long as I can remember, and most likely quite a while before that."

"You have a plan for that too?" Carroll asked, grinning.

"Only in very vague terms — you know, museum, conference center, something along those lines. It depends on how much work and money it would take to make it safe and usable."

"As always," Carroll admitted. "Is Josh still hanging around?"

I hoped I wasn't blushing. "Yes. His sabbatical year ends by September, and I guess he's going to have to find a new place to live around Baltimore. He says he likes the peace and quiet here. He's still working on something weighty about industrialization in the postbellum mid-Atlantic states."

"What did the factory make?"

"Shovels."

"Ah."

"Is that a good 'ah' or a bad 'ah'?" I had to ask.

"Well, it's reassuringly ordinary," Carroll said thoughtfully, "which means people can identify with it. On the other hand, a shovel is a shovel, and how much innovation can you apply to a shovel?"

"I keep hoping we'll find something in the documents that will explain everything."

"It's possible." Carroll jumped out of her chair. "Let's get started. Nell's been raving about the house, and I want to see if it lives up to her description."

"I was planning to head out there now. But it occurs to me it might be a good idea for you to see the town library first. Then you'll know what kind of processing space you'll have to work with. You might have to move the collection in stages."

"I guess that makes sense," Carroll said, but from her tone I had to think she'd rather see the original documents.

"Don't worry — the library's not far away, and it won't take long. Then we can head out to the mansion. Oh, did you bring a camera, just in case we find something juicy?"

"Of course. Onward!" Carroll said. "I'll go change clothes — digging through old collections is grubby work."

"Smart woman. Your room is first on the left at the top of the stairs," I told her.

While Carroll dressed, I put the dishes in the sink, closed the windows, and locked up the house, and when she returned I led Carroll to my car.

As we drove slowly down Main Street, I said, "You haven't seen the town before, have you?"

"Nope. I only know what Nell has told me. So this is the center of town?"

"Beginning, center, and end. If we were driving to the mansion — it's a few miles out of town — we'd turn left here. Too far to walk. Come on — the library's only a block or two away."

We reached the library in about two minutes, and I sorted through the keys to open the front door. Stepping in, the first thing I noticed was that there was a draft of cool morning air coming from somewhere. I hadn't noticed it the day before. I flipped the light switch and moved into the general area in front of the librarian's desk.

Carroll nudged my arm, then pointed.

"That window's broken," she said.

I followed her finger. Toward the back of the building, the perimeter was lined with six-foot wooden bookcases as old as the building. There were occasional transom windows in the space between the shelves and the top of the bookcases. I was sure the window hadn't been broken the day before. A break-in? Wouldn't it have been easier to get in through the back door, which no one could see from the street?

The space directly beneath that window was usually occupied by a wooden bookcase as old as the building. But now I couldn't see the bookcase directly under the window. I took a deep breath: time to check things out.

Carroll was right behind me. "You going to see what happened?" she asked.

"Well, I feel kind of responsible for the place. But I know I locked up when I left yesterday, and the door was locked when we got here, right?"

"It was. Let's do this, then. If it rains, books might get wet."

Trust Carroll to have her own priorities. Feeling a bit like a zombie, I walked toward the back wall, placing my feet carefully. Shards of glass began appearing on the floor about six feet away from the window. I reached the bookcase that had blocked my view and stepped around it. And saw a body lying on the floor.

# 9

Carroll bumped into me from behind, since I'd frozen where I was standing. When she peered around me, she said, "Wow, that's a body. Under a bookcase."

"Yes, it is. Are you going to throw up or anything?"

"No. I've been on some archeological digs with plenty of bodies, although they're usually older than this one — I can handle it. Anyone you know?"

"I can't swear to it, but I think he was here yesterday asking if he could come in and do some genealogy research. I told him to talk to the people at the town hall."

"You think he's dead?"

"There's an awful lot of blood on the floor, but I guess we should check." The man — body? — hadn't moved since we'd found it. I got as close as I dared, reached out a hand . . . and realized I didn't know what I was supposed to be looking for.

Where the heck was the relevant artery? I settled for laying my hand on the back of his neck, which was all that I could reach, what with the splintered bookcase and the scattered books. His neck was lukewarm, despite the summer heat. He wasn't breathing. He was dead.

I stood up carefully and backed away until I encountered a chair, and I dropped into it. Carroll followed suit in an adjoining chair. "This isn't your first body, is it?" she said gently.

"No. The first one was someone I'd known in high school, who I found on the steps on the mansion. Did I tell you about that? That was a lot more personal, though she hadn't been anything like a friend to me. This guy? I don't know him. I saw him exactly once, yesterday, if he even is the same guy. I told him what there was here and suggested he should go to the town hall this morning and ask for permission. I don't know if they've figured out a policy for what to do until they find a new librarian. If they're even looking for one. It's not exactly the most popular place in town. Then I watched him leave."

We sat in silence for a long minute. Then Carroll said, "What happens now? You call the local police?"

"The local police are not prepared to

handle homicides. If that's what this is. But usually they should be called first, and then they call the state police, who are about an hour away. The state guys are pretty competent, based on what I saw when I found Cordelia dead. I think I know a detective there well enough to call him directly. He may have considered me a suspect last time around, for about five minutes, but that didn't stick. I don't think he can pin this one on me."

"Then go ahead and call," Carroll said firmly.

"You want to go out to the mansion on your own and get started?" I asked tentatively.

"No. We found him together, so I'm a witness or something. And I think a death is more important that a bunch of old documents. They've been sitting in the attic for over a hundred years. A couple of more days won't hurt." She paused before asking, "Do you have an alibi for last night? Or since you last saw, uh, him?" She nodded toward the body.

"Actually, I do. After I watched this guy walk away, I went home and found Josh waiting on the steps. We had dinner. He left early this morning. So Detective Reynolds can't point toward me."

"Josh, huh? Anyway, do you have any idea why this person on the floor would have wanted to break into the town library?"

"He was looking for something, and I don't think it was his grandmother's marriage record." I stood up and walked away, then pulled out my cell phone. I knew I had left Detective Reynolds's number in its memory. I worried for a brief moment that he would refuse to take my call, or pass me on to someone junior to him, but once the receptionist heard my name, she put me through immediately.

"Kate Hamilton. You're still in Asheboro?" he asked. "You haven't found another body, have you?"

For a few moments I couldn't figure out a good way to answer that. Finally I said, "Actually, I have, in the town library."

"I'm on my way — I'll be there in half an hour," he said, and hung up.

I meandered back to where Carroll was sitting. I was surprised to see her staring at the wall over the body. "You talk to your police pal?" she asked.

"Yes. He's on his way. You want to sit somewhere else, like outside?"

"No. Actually, I've been thinking about the crime scene here," she said.

"Crime scene? Tell me you watch all the

procedural shows on television!"

"As often as I can. Now I can put what I've learned to good use."

"Great," I said, trying not to sound snide. "What can you tell me about the crime scene?"

"First, it seems kind of staged. Don't you think? It's supposed to look like he broke the window and climbed in, and after he had wormed his way inside he somehow pulled the bookcase over on top of him and it killed him. Ergo, accidental death."

"And you have doubts?"

"Yes, I do. For one, the way the glass is scattered looks kind of artificial — it's awfully tidy and evenly spread. Two, his head looks kind of lopsided and it seems to have bled a lot. I'll concede that may be the cause of death, but I cannot reconstruct any way the bookcase could have fallen over on top of him and hit his head in that particular spot. Which leads me to think that someone hit him with something, laid him out on the floor, and tipped the bookcase over on him. Do you see any problems with that?"

I considered. "Well, we don't know who he is — or was. We still aren't sure what he was doing here in Asheboro or the library. We have no idea why he would have thought breaking in, most likely in the middle of the night, was a good idea. And since we don't know who he is, we have no idea who might have wanted to kill him or for what reason or why they went to such lengths to make it look like an accident or what it has to do with Asheboro. So I guess I'll reserve judgment until I get some more information, which I hope the state police can provide."

"Fair enough," Carroll said agreeably.

We sat mostly in silence until a state police vehicle pulled up in front of the library. I went to the front door to open it. When the car doors opened, I said, "Detective Reynolds. I'd say it was nice to see you again, but I'd rather the circumstances were different."

"Kate, the feeling is mutual," he replied. "Have you called the local police?" When I shook my head, he added, "Let me talk to them, and then I can get your story."

We waited until he'd alerted the local police to his presence, and then he went to look at the body. The officer who had accompanied Detective Reynolds pulled out a camera and took lots of pictures — of the body, its position, its location within the building, the fallen bookcase, and apparently anything else he could think of. When he was done he nodded to the detective, who pulled on a pair of latex gloves and carefully turned the victim's head so he could see his face. I'd been right: it was my mystery man from the night before.

Detective Reynolds looked up at me. "You know this guy?"

I swallowed hard. "Yes and no. I don't know him personally or by name, but last night I was here to see how much room there was to transfer the Barton collection of documents over here to work on them, and he came to the door. He asked if he could come in — he said he was doing research on family history."

Reynolds stood up. "Did you let him in?"

"No. I just pointed to where the genealogy section is, so he could get a sense of how much material there might be, but then I told him that if he really wanted to use the library's collections, he should go plead his case to the town hall. I didn't think it was my place to give him free access, even though the mayor gave me the key, since there's no librarian at the moment and the library is closed until a replacement is found. He left, and I watched him go. Then I left myself, after I made sure all the doors were locked."

"He didn't say what he was looking for specifically?"

"No, just that he was looking for information about his family. He didn't give me the name."

The detective said carefully, "So late yesterday he was at the library asking questions, and this morning he's dead. That's one pretty big coincidence, Kate."

"Yes, it is. But that's all I know."

Detective Reynolds looked at me with a steady, level gaze. I was busy thanking the stars that he had caught this case, because it would save a lot of explaining — he knew the details of the last Asheboro death that I'd been associated with. I couldn't begin to explain about what was going on now, because I didn't understand what had happened.

I realized belatedly that Carroll hadn't said anything. "Detective, I apologize, but I never introduced Carroll Peterson here. She's works with historic documents in Philadelphia, and I asked her to come help me with the Barton collection. She arrived this morning."

Detective Reynolds turned to Carroll. "Have you been to Asheboro before, Ms. Peterson?"

"No. When Kate found the Barton papers, she took them to Philadelphia, which is where I saw them, and that's why she thought of me now."

"Did you know the deceased?"

"Never saw him before. Listen, can I ask you something?" Carroll said.

"Regarding this death? All right."

"Do you think this was an accident, or was he murdered?"

I could swear that the detective almost smiled. "And why would you ask that?"

"Because there's no way he could have crawled in through the window and fallen with the bookcase on top of him bashing his head."

"I'll take that under consideration." He turned back to me. "I'm going to have to declare this building a crime scene, and I'll ask you not to use it until it's cleared with me."

"You just called it a crime scene, even though there's no proof that there's a crime," I said. "Does that mean you agree with Carroll? The guy was murdered? He didn't just happen to hit his head?"

"Possibly," he said.

"Will you tell us what the medical examiner has to say?" I asked.

"In confidence, for now. But I know I can trust you. Will you be remaining at that place in town where you stayed last time?"

"Yes, although if it's all right I think Carroll and I will be going out to the Barton mansion to begin cataloging the records there. You can reach me by phone if you need anything else."

"I have no problem with that. I'll let you know when I learn anything definitive."

"Thank you. Oh, do you want the keys to the library?"

"That would be helpful."

I retrieved the key ring from my bag and handed it over. "I'd like the keys back when you're finished. We may still want to use this space." If I could erase the mental image of a bloody corpse. Carroll didn't seem to be having that problem.

"Understood. We'll talk later." I could feel him watching us as Carroll and I left by the front door.

# 10

"I need to get my car — it's still at the B&B," I told Carroll.

"Oh, right — we walked to the library," Carroll said. She must have been more rattled by the body than I had thought.

Actually, I was glad of the chance to walk, to sort out my thoughts. Another body, and I had to be the one to find it. Had somebody planned that, or was it just an awful coincidence? No one could blame me for the death of a stranger, and yet, there I was with another body. People would be wondering.

"Kate? We're here at the B&B," Carroll said.

"Oh, right. Do you need anything from inside, or are you good to go?"

"I packed up the car earlier. And we don't need to finish everything today — this is just to evaluate what's there and what kind of time we'll need. You okay to drive?"

"Sure. I really need the distraction, and

I've been looking forward to showing you Henry's property and the house. So let's go."

In the car I retraced our path toward town and made the turn I'd shown Carroll. Then I proceeded at a leisurely rate until we approached the front gate.

"Okay, where is it?" Carroll asked impatiently.

"About a half mile thataway." I waved vaguely to the right. "It's carefully positioned to provide privacy. Just wait for it."

I opened the gate, drove through, then stopped again and locked the gate. When I climbed back into the car, Carroll said, "You have problems with trespassers here? Or vandals?"

"I think most people have forgotten this place exists, particularly since no one can see it from the road. But there's no point in making it easy for someone to sneak in. There are some rudimentary alarms inside the house, but they're not enough to stop someone who's really determined. And it's easy to find a way to sneak onto the land, because except for the gate here, the fence is a joke. I speak from experience."

I slowed just a bit, to build up the arrival of the first view of the mansion. When we reached the crest of the hill, I stopped to let

Carroll take in the view.

"Wow," she said, barely above a whisper. She was silent for maybe thirty seconds as she took in the vista in front of her. "I see what Nell meant. And it still has all its original furnishings?"

"It does. Mostly Tiffany studios, with a dash of William Morris. In good condition."

"Brilliant. Of course, there are some people who don't like the Victorian style," Carroll said dubiously.

"Tell them to stay home, or go watch fake soldiers shooting at each other with fake guns on some battlefield. Me, I'm fighting to save this place and to get it the admiration it deserves," I said firmly.

Carroll grinned. "Where do I sign up?"

"Stick with me." I drove around the side of the building. Josh's car was in its usual place, but he didn't come out to greet us, even though he was expecting us this morning. Maybe he and his guest, Alison, were engaged in hot, steamy . . . no, I wasn't going to go there. I hadn't even seen the woman, and she could be a crone. Or married. Still, I figured we'd better find out sooner rather than later, and got out of the car, and so did Carroll.

Finally Josh came tromping down the outside stairs of the carriage house. "Hey,

Kate. And you're Carroll, right? I'm glad you could make it. Are you looking forward to this?" I noticed he didn't try to explain what had taken him so long. But I didn't see Alison either.

"Do you really need to ask?" Carroll said, smiling at him. "A collection of documents that hasn't been seen for, what, over a hundred years? What library science student wouldn't be drooling by now?"

"Then let's get started," Josh told her. "Kate filled you in on the history of the house?"

"She did, although I already knew much of it from the last time she and I met. I hope the two of you didn't make too much of a mess in the attic when you found Clara's letters."

"We were very careful," Josh said seriously. "Besides, it was Cordelia who went rooting around in there first. We can blame any mess on her, because Kate and I were careful. So, where do you want to start?"

"I want to get a sense of the scope of the collection before I look at anything specific," Carroll told him. "You have any idea what linear footage you have up there?"

Josh shrugged. "I'd say a couple of hundred feet. It's hard to tell, since everything is stored in wooden boxes or trunks, and we don't know how full they are. The attic takes up most of the third story of the house. But things are kind of jumbled, and there are some assorted pieces of old furniture as well, so I'm really just guessing."

"Any damage problems?" Carroll demanded. "Leaks in the roof? Rodents? Mold?"

"Not that I've seen," Josh said. "As Kate may have told you, when Henry died, no family member wanted the place, so in his will he left it to the town, expecting them to sell it. Luckily he left more than adequate funds to take care of it until it sold, although I'm sure he didn't expect that no one would be interested and he thought it would sell quickly. Thank goodness the town took Henry's terms seriously, and spent the funds keeping it in good shape. There was plenty of money left, until the local bank president appropriated most of it for his own ends."

Carroll grinned. "And here Kate said life was dull in these parts! A murder, embezzlement — and now another murder."

"What?" Josh said.

"I'll explain once we get Carroll started in the attic," I told him. "She already knows. Where's your houseguest?"

"She has a room at the hotel and would

rather stay there. I think she disapproved of my housekeeping standards."

"Have you told her anything about the papers in the attic?"

"Of course not. We don't even know what's in them, and I doubt they fall in her area of interest. Why do you want to know?" Josh protested.

I sighed. "I'll have to explain."

"Will you two stop bickering so we can get started?" Carroll interrupted. "Or maybe you can stay down here and Kate can explain while I make the first pass in the attic."

Josh looked confused but didn't protest. "I'll take you up," I told her.

I found the key to the front door in my bag and led the way around the house — I wanted to give Carroll the best possible view. When I opened the door I let her enter first, then waited.

Her reaction wasn't long in coming. "Oh my God!" she whispered. She walked to the middle of the hallway and turned in a full circle. "Nell wasn't kidding! This is amazing. Can you show me the rest?"

"Of course," I said. I took her on the brief tour of the ground floor, because I was pretty sure she was still eager to get to the attic. When we came back to the main hall,

I told her, "We can go through it in more detail later, but I think you need to see the attic so we can begin planning. There's nothing of much interest in the bedrooms."

"I know, I know," she said absently, but it took her another minute before she could tear herself away from admiring the magnificent Victorian décor. "Lead on."

As we trudged up the handsome mahogany staircase to the second floor, I asked her, "When will we be able to move the stuff out?"

"It depends on how much there is, and if it's all documents rather than table linens or china. What's the hurry? We aren't sure when we'll be able to get back into the library."

"You're right. And that reminds me — I'd better tell the mayor, or his assistant, that we aren't sure when we're going to need some willing people to help us carry stuff. And maybe a van. Just go do what you do best and we'll figure it out later in the day."

"Great," Carroll said. "Now point me to the attic."

For all of her eagerness to get started, it was hard to get Carroll to move quickly. We wandered down the main hall toward the attic entrance, with Carroll oohing and aahing every few feet at some elaborate architectural detail. "Are the books in the library downstairs part of the collection?" she asked.

"We really don't know, but you can take a look at them. But right now we're here for the attic."

"I guess," she sighed. "Lead on."

"This way," Josh said, and led the way along the second-floor hallway. When he reached the door that led to the attic he pulled out his own ring of keys from the pocket of his jeans and opened the door, then held it for Carroll to enter. I followed the two of them.

The door to the attic was located at the midpoint of the hallway, so at the top of the attic stairs you could turn either left or right. I knew that Clara's letters had been located halfway down the space on the left, toward the front of the house, and that was about all I'd had the chance to explore. I had no idea if there was any order to all the stuff up there, and I didn't know if Josh had done more poking around since then, but this didn't seem to be the right time to ask. When Carroll reached the top of the stairs she stopped and said, "That's far enough."

"Huh?" Josh said, clearly confused.

"I don't need you two bumbling around up here. Let me get a sense of what's what and get an idea of what needs to be done, and then we can confer."

Josh glanced at me, and I nodded. "We don't know anything about what's up here, Carroll," I admitted, "since the Clara Barton papers are gone, so I guess we'd only get in the way. We'll be downstairs."

Carroll had already turned to the boxes in the attic, looking like a kid in a candy shop, so Josh and I dutifully trooped down the stairs again, and stood hesitating in the hallway.

"Well," he began, "she certainly knows what she wants."

"That she does. But Nell vouches for her, so she must be good at what she does. And you know if we stuck our noses in, we'd get distracted in a minute and probably mislay or damage stuff."

"Look, I get it," Josh said, although he still sounded miffed. "But I don't think we should leave her alone in the building. We can wait downstairs. So, are you going to tell me about this new murder?"

"You mean the body in the library? Sounds like an Agatha Christie novel, but unfortunately it's true. We went over there to check out how much space there was for us to work on the cataloging and found someone dead inside."

"Good God," Josh said. "Are you all right?"

"I don't really know yet. Carroll was with me. We made sure he was dead, and I called Detective Reynolds. He was still there when we left to come out here."

"Anybody you know?"

"Not exactly. It was the young guy I told you about last night, the one who wanted to work on his family history."

"And now he's dead?" Josh asked, sounding incredulous.

"He is most definitely dead. It appears that he broke in through one of those high windows on the side of the building, and somehow got bashed by a rather large old bookcase."

"Appears?"

I chose my words carefully. "Carroll and I believe that it was made to look like he came in that way, and Detective Reynolds more or less agreed that the death wasn't natural. He called the library a crime scene, and shooed Carroll and me out."

"That is deeply troubling. I'm sorry you had to see it."

"So am I." I kind of shook myself. "Detective Reynolds said he'd call when he had any more information about the person."

"Which means he doesn't suspect you."

"Why would he? Just because I found Cordelia dead — something I had nothing to do with — why would he assume I was involved in killing this stranger?"

"I didn't mean to imply . . . I'm sorry. You've just hit a patch of bad luck, and it's not your fault. What can I do?"

"I wish I knew. But, Josh? Thanks for caring."

"Anytime, Kate. So, what now?"

"I guess we're waiting for Carroll to finish her first pass. And waiting for Detective Reynolds to tell us what he's found out, like a name for the victim. Are you going to get together with Alison?"

"We left it open, but I don't want to get in your way, and I don't have anything to contribute to the investigation, beyond saying I haven't seen any uninvited strangers here. Nor have I noticed any break-ins or missing items. Although I am your alibi for last night, if Reynolds wants it."

"We'll see."

# 11

Josh left the room to call Alison, wherever she was, and came back to tell me that they'd arranged to meet at the carriage house, and then they were going to lunch at the hotel. That left me on my own, at loose ends. Carroll was still in the attic, but without a car of her own, since I'd brought her to the estate. But then she'd told me to stay out of her way while she went through the documents for the first time, so I had no idea how long she might be, and if the detective didn't release the crime scene, there was no need to hurry. I'd have loved to explore the mansion some more, but like Carroll, I wanted to approach it systematically.

Of course, when it came to actually refurbishing it I'd hire a high-end design firm, but I wanted to get a personal sense of what needed to be done if I was going to work with them. I already knew that my primary goal was to change as little as possible, and if something was too far deteriorated to preserve, I'd argue to replace it with an exact replica. I could envision a lot of head-to-head battles with whatever firm I ended up with, but I was prepared to stand my ground. Assuming, of course, I could find the money to pay for it all. If the project even happened. All these bodies were kind of messing things up.

I'd borrowed a lined pad from Josh and settled myself at the dining room table to make some notes about what needed doing in the mansion, but my mind kept wandering back to the young man's body. He'd been alive yesterday, and today he was dead. Why?

Asheboro is a small town, and few strangers end up in it without a reason. Okay, the kid had given a reason: genealogy. While I'd never felt the need to explore my own family tree, I recognized that it was a popular hobby, and despite the huge strides in online databases, there were plenty of original sources hidden away in dusty file boxes or filing cabinets in small, local historical societies and libraries. I was willing to concede that finding obscure records like that could have been the guy's only goal. I felt badly about turning him away, but too many odd things were happening in town to trust a stranger, much less let him roam freely in the library.

He'd left and I had no idea where he'd been staying, nor had I asked him how to reach him if I found a way to let him into the library — I'd leave that to the state police to check. He was not my problem, or so I had thought. But that was before I'd found his body. Of course he could have slept in a motel a town or two over, or maybe in his car — if he had one. Again, the detective could follow up on that.

As far as I knew, so far, the poor young man didn't have a name — he hadn't bothered to introduce himself. I had no idea where he'd come from. That just seemed wrong to me. If you are confronted with a body, it's an intimate thing, and you'd like to know the who and the why. At least I trusted Detective Reynolds to find out.

I wasn't getting a lot done, and I hoped that Carroll had made some progress. I'd given her two or three hours of uninterrupted time to grub around in the attic — maybe it was time to see if she'd come up with anything. I trekked up the staircase and knocked at the attic door before calling out, "Carroll, you still up there?"

I heard a distant "Yes," so I added, "I'm

coming up."

"Come ahead."

I climbed the stairs and spotted Carroll at the far end of the attic, toward the front. She'd started where the Clara Barton letters had been? Was that a good sign? She stood up and stretched, then pushed her hair out of her face. "I've finished about one-quarter so far, although from the few labels I've seen a lot of the remaining boxes may contain household goods rather than papers."

"Are you recording them? Because they might be useful somewhere else."

"Of course. I take notes on everything. Are you ready to go?"

"If you are. Josh has gone off to brainstorm with Alison, but we can give him a summary later, if he wants one."

"Any word from the state police?"

"Not yet. But the detective said he'd call when he knew anything, and he's pretty reliable. I hate to say it, but I got bored downstairs. You've got something constructive to do, but I feel like I can't really start anything until I know more. I may have to go back to talking to the shopkeepers in town."

"Isn't that important?"

"Yes, of course it is, but it's not my strong suit. Have you found anything useful? As in, something that I can use?"

"Not really, but I've barely scratched the surface. Last time you were poking around here, did you see any records about the factory?"

"Here? Or at the library?"

"Anywhere," she said. "Because they're conspicuously absent from anything up here. Henry seems to have kept good records, so I'm surprised there's not a stack of factory information. You know, production amounts, payrolls, that kind of thing. I bet Josh would drool if we found anything like that."

"Do you know, I've been thinking along the same lines. Clara's letters make it clear that Henry needed the funds from his inheritance to buy this place and maybe set up the factory. But that would have been right after the Civil War. I think he went way beyond that, but I'm just guessing. I can't imagine that the shovel factory would generate enough income to decorate this house, so there must have been some other source."

"I think so too," Carroll said, "but I haven't seen the evidence. But it's early days yet. Right now I'm hot, dusty, and seeing cross-eyed. Probably a good time to call it quits. We can start again early in the morning. There's definitely enough to keep me busy for another day or two, if your detective doesn't let us into the library."

"Sounds good to me."

As I led the way back down the stairs, then turned off the light and locked the door once Carroll was clear, I realized I'd kind of been hoping that Carroll would find something important right away. I'd already given myself the lecture about how unlikely it was, but I needed something tangible to hang my plan on. Just assembling a nice ordinary Victorian town wasn't exactly a draw for visitors. I needed something that people would recognize and would consider worthy of a trip to the town. I kept trying to convince myself that Asheboro was not all that far from Baltimore and would be convenient for people traveling the Civil War circuit, but I didn't think a couple of dead bodies would garner the right kind of publicity, and if we didn't find anything better, that would be all that the general public would remember.

Once downstairs, Carroll went out the back door and inhaled deeply. "Better," she declared. "I mean, I love the smell of old paper and leather and even mildew, but oxygen is kind of necessary now and then." She sat down on the back steps, and I joined her. "What're the plans for the evening?" she asked.

"I don't have any. I don't know if Josh has any food at his place. I don't even know if he'll be around this evening. He hasn't said how long Alison is staying. I haven't even seen her yet."

"You jealous?"

"I don't know. Josh and I aren't exactly . . . I don't know what. I've only known him a month or so. He's divorced but hasn't been for long, and I don't think he's sticking around here when his sabbatical is over. So I really can't say where things are going with us."

I stood up and stretched, wandering over to sit on a low stone wall. Carroll stayed on the steps, jotting notes in a small notebook. "What's your general impression of the documents, based on what you've seen up to now?" I asked.

She looked up from her scribbling. "That Henry — or whoever was working for him — was methodical and thorough, at least with the stuff I've looked at so far. Every now and then he mentions his wife, but it's always brief, like, 'Mary had a bad day today.' Sad when you think about it. He had all this money — that he'd earned himself — but his wife was apparently too ill to enjoy it, and you can't even see the nearest neighbor from here, and there were no children to leave any of it to. Tell me something: Was he a manager or did he take an active part in his business? Because he didn't seem to have a lot else in his life."

"I have no idea, actually. Josh might know. Or there might be something at the library about his life and his role at the factory. I can't imagine what he could have done with shovels, though. No moving parts, even."

"Maybe he did something more than make shovels? Josh should definitely have a handle on that. Oh, sorry — bad pun."

"I forgive you. As I said, I don't know if he — or they — will want to eat with us tonight. Since I don't know what Alison's area of specialization is, I have no idea if what we're doing would interest her. Or if she had anything to share that would be useful to us."

"Well, if you see her, go ahead and invite her and we can find out," Carroll said firmly. She stared out at the view for a couple of minutes, thinking. Finally she said, "Okay, for argument's sake, let's assume that Henry had a secret that he kept well hidden. Something that nobody knew about."

"That he never shared? What? Professional? Social? What would require concealing back in 1880 something?" I asked, getting into the spirit of our game.

"I don't know. He already had plenty of money. He doesn't seem to have traveled much. Could he have been smuggling something? Or maybe he ran the biggest brothel in western Maryland."

"I doubt it," I told her. "If it was smuggling, there's no transport — no train line, and the carriage house here couldn't have held more than two horses and a couple of carriages, which is not exactly enough to carry out a major smuggling organization, and who would want to bother with a small one? If it was a brothel, I can't imagine there were enough customers around to make it worthwhile. Leaving aside what Mary would have thought of it, unless she was demented and wouldn't notice. Maybe he was a mad scientist with a state-of-the-art lab in the basement and was working on some wonderful new discovery, but either it didn't work out, or the death of his wife drove him into such a depression that he lost interest and abandoned it."

"We're nuts, you know," Carroll said, smiling. "We're sitting here making up fantastical stories about a man we know very little about, and we have absolutely no evidence of anything. Have you been in the basement?"

"Only briefly. It was dark, and I couldn't see much of anything. I only wanted to be sure it wasn't damp or infested with giant spiders."

"Was it?"

"Not that I could see."

"Maybe we should check it out."

"Hey, you're supposed to be cataloging!" I reminded her.

"Yes, but I've had enough for one day. I can only take so many hours of inhaling dust."

"And the basement would be better?"

"We can find out."

"So let's do it. Then there will be two of us to fight the spiders."

# 12

I was rummaging through my keys, looking for one that would open the basement door, when my cell phone rang: Detective Reynolds. I held up one finger to Carroll, then answered the call.

"Detective! Do you have good news for me?"

"News, yes. Good? Well . . ."

"Just tell me, please. Have you identified the victim?"

"The young man was Zachary Mitchell, from New Jersey, according to his driver's license. He was twenty-five. He had a student ID showing that he was a graduate student at Johns Hopkins, although we haven't discovered what department. That's where Josh is employed, correct?"

"Yes. He's not here at the moment, but he should be back later, and you can ask whether he knew this Zachary person."

"I'll be doing that. In any case, we're still

looking for Mr. Mitchell's car, if he came in one, and trying to identify where he might have been staying. If he hadn't just arrived, that is. It would have been an easy trip from Baltimore for him, and maybe he wasn't planning to stay over."

"Do you know yet how he died?" I asked, not sure whether I'd get an answer.

"This is off the record for now. The preliminary examination suggests that you were right: the blow to the back of the head was the cause of death, and there was no way the bookcase could have inflicted that. Somebody staged the scene."

"I assume your people are doing all the obvious things, like looking for fingerprints on the glass and bookcase."

"Of course. Let me ask you this: Was anything disturbed inside the library? Or missing?"

"Are you asking if he — or his killer — actually did get in and used the time to hunt for . . . whatever it is they're hunting for?"

"Yes. To repeat myself, was there any evidence that someone had made it into the building, before or after killing Mr. Mitchell?"

"I wasn't looking for anything, but I'd say no. No one has been inside since Audrey left, and she kept things neat. Plus someone might have noticed if there were a flashlight bobbing around inside the building. When do you think he was killed?"

"Hard to say with any certainty. You make a good point: it would have been hard to move things around in the dark. Possibly at sunrise? I assume there would not be many people on the streets then."

"Probably not. But I should point out that there were adjustable blinds inside the library, to protect the books from being damaged by sunlight. While a moving flashlight might still have been visible, predawn seems more likely. And the body was still slightly warm when Carroll and I arrived. Had anyone else in town seen him or talked to him?"

"We haven't had the opportunity to ask the local people yet. We'll be doing that later today, or tomorrow."

I was sure the detective was a busy man. "Are you officially calling this a murder?"

"I'm afraid so. Don't spread that around, though. Say for public consumption that he was killed by a falling bookcase, and ask if anyone knows why he might have been in the library."

"Fine. Oh, and can we use the library? I mean, have you cleared it?"

"Give us the rest of the day, and you may

use it tomorrow."

I felt a surge of relief. "Thank you. You'll let me know if you learn anything else?"

"If and when I can. And tell Mr. Wainwright that I'd like to talk with him."

"I'll do that. Thanks again."

Carroll had been silently watching our exchanges. "So we're good to go?"

"Looks like it. The poor guy turns out to be Zachary Mitchell, graduate student at Johns Hopkins. And you were right; his death was not accidental. And that's all he told me. You ready to tackle the basement now?"

"Lead on."

I found the right key to the cellar door on the second try, and it swung open, releasing a wave of damp air.

"Do you have a flashlight?" Carroll asked.

"Uh, no — only the one on my cell phone. But we're not excavating King Tut's tomb. We're just checking out what's down there and whether it's worth exploring. If we think we've found something important, we can come back later, when we're better prepared. And remind me to find some more flashlights and leave them in the car."

"Let's go, then!" Carroll said with enthusiasm. Carroll was proving to be a great sidekick, except when she told me to leave her alone to work. I could live with that.

Standing in the doorway, I remembered a lonely single electric lightbulb from my last and only visit to the cellar, and I'll admit I held my breath when I flipped the switch at the top of the stairs. The bulb lit up, not that the room was much brighter than it had been.

"What are we looking for?" Carroll whispered.

"Why are you whispering?" I answered in a normal voice. "We're the only people in the house. I hope."

"So you go first."

"Chicken," I told Carroll with a smile.

The basement was much as I remembered it: large, dark, and dirty. Cobwebs hung from the floor joists only a few inches above our heads. How tall had Henry been? I had to wonder. "Hey, don't Civil War military records include a person's height? We might be able to figure out how tall Henry was."

"I think you're right. They should be online. Should we guess that he wasn't worried about bumping his head down here?"

"That's what I was wondering." Once my eyes adjusted, I saw that the space, which extended the full length and breadth of the house, did include a few enclosed areas. I told Carroll, "The last time I was down here, I realized that Henry had incorporated portions of what was the original farmhouse when he expanded the house — you can see where the masonry changes in the foundation. And one of those enclosed spaces" — I pointed — "was a root cellar, I think."

"What about the others?" Carroll asked as she looked around.

"That I can't tell you. Last time there really wasn't any reason to stay down here too long, once I was sure the place was structurally sound."

"Big furnace," Carroll commented.

"It's a big house. But it comes with its own tools!" I pointed to a cluster of long metal things I assumed were coal pokers or scrapers or something like that. They were too big to be much else.

"So what are we looking for?" Carroll asked. "The alchemist's lair?"

"Got me. I don't spend a lot of time in Victorian basements, so I don't know what typical is. Clearly it's not a laundry room. But let's think logically. How much space would Henry have wanted for his activities down here?"

"Kate, that is a ridiculous question," Carroll declared. "Maybe we need to look at it from the opposite direction: What *could*

Henry do down here, based on its size and utilities? We need to narrow the field. Do you see him as a furniture maker or a jeweler?"

"Not really. I think he was more practical and more intelligent than those hobbies would call for, although maybe he liked to work with his hands. But in general, from what you've seen of his papers, would you agree?"

"Yes, I think so, although it's an incomplete sample. Photographer? Photo developing was still pretty new in those days, and it would have been challenging to him. But I haven't found any photographs in the attic, except a few studio portraits, although he could have kept his own work in the library or some other room in the house."

"I'd love to see a picture of Henry. And his wife," I said wistfully. "Maybe the library has some."

Carroll went on, "Besides, it's too dusty in the basement, particularly with a coal furnace. All the photos would be covered with imperfections, and if the interior upstairs is any guide, Henry was meticulous. He wouldn't want dust specks all over his pictures."

"Carroll, I'm running out of ideas," I told her. "The timing is wrong for a model train set. The ceiling is too low for him to set up an exercise area. Or a boxing ring, because he'd need someone else to spar with."

"Maybe you're not thinking big enough."

"What do you mean?" I asked.

"What if the whole space was a laboratory? Apart from the furnace and the coal for it, of course."

"The whole basement? What would he have been doing with that much space?"

"Making something big. That would be measured in feet, not inches. Maybe he was building a boat. And don't say shovels, because that would require melting metal, and this basement is not *that* big. Or well vented."

"This is kind of fun, even if we don't come up with any answers," I told Carroll. "Are there scientific tests to determine what residues were left behind? You know — like wood scraps, metal shavings, glass shards, and so on? Or weird chemicals?"

"Maybe." Carroll glanced quickly at her watch. "I don't think we're going to find the answer tonight, but at least we have something to think about. How about we pick this up again in the morning, after we've had time to think about it?"

"Fine, but what about the cataloging?" I protested.

"I'll work on that tomorrow, and you can poke around down here and I'll join you when I burn out in the attic. Give me another day or two and we should be ready to transfer it all to the library, now that your detective has given the go-ahead."

"Works for me."

When we went back up the stairs, Josh was banging around in the kitchen. Carroll and I headed in that direction. He looked surprised to see us. "I thought you'd be . . . somewhere else."

"Nope. Carroll had enough of the attic — it's hot and dusty up there — so we went down to the basement to look around."

"Find anything interesting?"

"A lot of space. Now we're wondering what Henry might have been doing with it. If anything. Is Alison coming back for dinner?"

"No, she said she had plans, but we're supposed to meet again in the morning. Have you heard from Reynolds?"

"Yes. He has a name for the dead man. Oh, and he wants to talk to you, because he said the guy — whose name was Zachary Mitchell — had a student ID that said he was a grad student at Johns Hopkins, and he wondered if you might know him."

"Doesn't sound familiar, but I'll be happy

to talk to him."

"Good. And he said we could go ahead and transfer our files to the library in town, starting tomorrow. The police are done with it."

"Did he find any evidence that anything was taken or disturbed?" Josh asked.

"No. So we still don't know why this Zachary was here, and why he's dead."

"May I remind you that we aren't detectives?" Josh said with a hint of sarcasm. "There's a perfectly fine detective and who knows how many people working for the state police looking into this. Can we just get back to what we're supposed to be doing? Carroll, have you found anything in the attic files worth reporting?"

"Mostly the absence of anything particularly noteworthy," she replied. "No more finds like the Clara Barton letters, at least so far. But I thought the total lack of any information or files on Henry's factory and its operations rather interesting. Henry was an almost compulsive recordkeeper, so why no factory records?"

"Did someone remove them?" Josh asked, looking interested in spite of himself.

"It doesn't look like anything is missing from the attic — no gaps, no sign of anything being dragged out. If the records were there and were removed, it was a long time ago. Assuming that Henry himself didn't destroy them all before he died. But I don't know why he'd do that."

"Huh," Josh said intelligently. "What about in the factory itself?"

Ah, yes, that was the question. "That's what Carroll and I wondered," I said. "I can get the keys to that building, if I don't already have them — thanks to the bank and the town hall, I seem to have a *lot* of keys. I think it's worth investigating."

"My gut says there have to be records somewhere," Carroll said firmly.

I nodded. "I agree, so that's two votes."

"I wouldn't miss it," Josh said quickly.

I turned to Carroll. "How much longer do you think it will take you to finish the preliminary assessment of what's in the attic?"

"Now that I've seen them all, I'd quess another day, maybe, although it won't be very detailed. But it's just the first pass. I can go into more details once we've moved them."

I thought for a moment. "I don't know if the mayor can pull together a moving crew by Sunday, although I can ask. If he can't, we can go look at the factory then. If he can, we'll put the factory off until Monday, or maybe there'll be time to do them both on one day. I'm glad you'll be coming with us, Josh, because whatever equipment is left in the building, I doubt I'd recognize whatever it was. So, Josh, what are you doing about dinner?"

"Me? Well, if you insist, there's always spaghetti. And maybe some wine."

"Sounds good to me."

# 13

It didn't take long to finish the spaghetti, and there was no dessert. Josh had found a bottle of wine in the fridge and we finished that among us. I was glad I'd stopped after the second glass of wine, because I wasn't making sense even to myself. I could tell Carroll was fading too and had worked in the stuffy attic for most of the day. "Carroll, you ready to go back to town?"

She pulled her eyes open with some effort. "Definitely. Then back to the mansion in the morning?"

"Yes. Josh, are you meeting Alison again? Oh, and I should ask, would she be likely to know anything that might help me with the town project? I'd like to meet her."

"We can work here at the carriage house, and then maybe you two can get together."

"That would be great. Once Carroll figures out how much stuff we'll have to move into town, I can talk to Mayor Skip about lining up people to help."

"And you're going to let Detective Reynolds and his merry band solve the murder without your help?"

"I've got plenty to keep me busy. But I reserve the right to poke my nose into it if it turns out that Zachary Mitchell was hunting for something that relates to Henry Barton. I know more about Henry and his history than the police department does."

"I'll concede that," Josh said. "You know, it's possible the Clara Barton find did attract some attention, and this Mitchell guy thought he was on the trail of something. You're digging into stuff that hasn't been touched in over a century. The public — or at least academics and people who actually read these days — know we found the Barton letters, and they might wonder whatever else you'll find. Maybe they're looking for something specific that they have reason to believe is there, but they didn't think of it before all this publicity started."

"You never thought about it?" I demanded, incredulously. "I mean, you specialize in nineteenth-century history, right? Shouldn't you have heard of Henry Barton through your own research? You've been living on his property!"

"Maybe, but this town is not exactly

mainstream. And to be honest, when this caretaker post popped up, it seemed like a gift from heaven — a quiet spot with few distractions, smack in the middle of a geographic area that I was already researching, with few demands. I never looked at it as research material."

I wondered briefly how difficult his divorce had been, so much so that he'd run across the state to get away from the memories. "So you don't have a clue about what the heck Henry Barton was into? Successful industrialist at a time when the country was booming, after the Civil War, and he wasn't the only success story. Was he just lucky? Or is there something we haven't seen yet?"

"I think the second is more likely. And all this trouble started when the news of the Clara letters went public, and the world realized we were looking at the old records nobody had known existed. Now you're saying that there's nothing startling in the attic of the mansion except for the omission of anything to do with how Henry made his money, and if you ask me, the answer has to be the factory. You and Carroll are going to sort out all his papers from the attic over the next few days, and I'll do some digging into what was going on in this particular part of the state, and then we'll take on the factory. There must be a record somewhere."

"Josh, do you think the dead man was looking for something specific in the library? Or someone else was — someone who was willing to kill for whatever it might be? I know it sounds far-fetched, but one person is already dead."

Josh smiled ruefully. "Seems ridiculous, doesn't it? But as you point out, it seems possible. Can you defend yourself?"

"What, like with a weapon? Or karate? Of course not — and I've never needed to, even in Philadelphia and Baltimore. How about you? Is there a gun in your apartment, or in the mansion, for that matter?"

"Not that I know of, and I wouldn't know what to do with one anyway. So the short answer is yes, we may be vulnerable. Although I think Reynolds is smart enough to realize that a second murder associated with the mansion looks pretty suspicious."

"I can't imagine that Cordy's death is related to Zachary's, but there's still something suspicious about it, and the common link seems to be Henry Barton." My brain was getting fuzzy, and I tried to pull myself together. "I'm sorry — it's been a long day and I'm tired, and I'm sure Carroll is too. I may be seeing killers behind every tree. But

I do think we should all be careful. Carroll and I will go straight to the mansion in the morning and see if we can get through the rest of the documents, so I can set up getting them moved to the library. And then we'll take on the factory."

"Who knows what lurks in that old building? I may get a publication out of it."

I stood up, and nudged Carroll, whose eyelids were drooping. "Just take care, will you?" I leaned in for a quick good-night kiss, but Josh stretched it out, and damn, it felt good. I finally managed to pull away. "Good night."

I headed for the door, followed by Carroll. Outside, she raised one eyebrow at me.

I answered her unspoken question. "Ask me in three months, if this insane project gets off the ground. Let's go!"

The drive back to town was uneventful. As we left the Barton property I made sure to lock the gate behind us. Maybe that was naïve of me. These days any teenage kid with a smartphone and enough time unobserved could probably override the code and sneak in without anybody noticing, and without leaving a trail. And there was nothing I could do about it, short of blowing the budget on surveillance cameras. Or attack dogs.

When Carroll and I got back to the B&B, everything appeared calm. I'd made sure all the timers on the lights were working, so the building looked welcoming — and safe. I unlocked the door and let Carroll in, then locked the door behind us. "You want a late snack? We never did get dessert."

"Don't bother. I'm ready to fall over, and we should get an early start in the morning if we want to finish with the attic."

"You are too sensible, but you're right. I think your room has everything you'll need. I've never managed a place this small before. I do better ordering things in the hundreds and having my staff take care of distributing them."

"Are you saying there won't be a mint on my pillow?"

"Hey, at least you've got a pillow. And sheets!"

"Good night, Kate." Carroll turned and walked up the stairs. Staring at her back, I wondered whether, if she had known what she was walking into in Asheboro, she would have declined my invitation.

I figured I might as well go to bed too. As I was doing a walk-through of the ground floor, making sure windows were closed and no taps were running and turning off lights, I noticed there was a message light flashing on the landline. I considered ignoring it, but I realized it could be Detective Reynolds again, and whatever he might tell us could affect our plans for the next few days, so I picked up. To my surprise it wasn't the detective; it was Ryan.

I pushed Play, and heard Ryan's voice. "Kate, sorry I missed you. I've got a favor to ask. An old college friend of mine is taking a few days to wander the battlefields, and I told him I knew a delightful bed-and-breakfast in a quaint and charming town. I know it's an imposition, but could you put him up for a couple of nights? He's house-trained and very polite. And I'll owe you one. I'll call you early tomorrow and confirm."

If I'd had any energy I would have fumed at his presumption. Imposition? You think? Of course, maybe he didn't know about the murder investigation. So all there was on my plate for tomorrow was to help catalog a collection of nineteenth-century correspondence, corral the mayor and his people to move the whole thing to the library over the next couple of days, and then hunt for something we weren't sure existed but quite possibly some mysterious other people thought was important. Oh, and help solve yet another murder. Piece of cake, right?

I followed Carroll's route up the stairs and fell into bed.

Nothing dire happened during the night. I woke up, stretched, and lay listening for any sound of movement from Carroll's room next door. Oops — the only sounds I heard — apart from birds — were coming from the kitchen below, and there went the distinctive whirr of my coffee grinder. I guessed it was time to get up.

I grabbed a quick shower, threw on something that could withstand shoving stuff around the attic, and wandered downstairs. "You're up early," I said when I reached the kitchen door.

"Good morning to you too," Carroll said, looking surprisingly cheerful. "Sleep well?"

"I did. No nightmares about madmen — or madwomen — lurking about, looking for a few pieces of paper. You found all the coffee supplies?"

"Of course I did. I am trained in finding things."

"Good. Oh, before I forget, there was a call on the landline here from my long-ago heartthrob Ryan — long story, or have you already heard it before? Anyway, technically Ryan owns this property, but he graciously let his ex-wife, Cordelia, manage it as a bed-

and-breakfast."

"You mean dead Cordelia, right?"

"The same. But apparently Ryan still feels he has a certain claim on the place. He called to tell me he'd offered a room to an old college friend who's touring the battlefields and was looking for an idyllic place to stay, so of course he thought of this place. Obviously I didn't have the opportunity to tell him we've had a murder in town, and housekeeping, much less for a place with six bedrooms, was never my strong suit. But Ryan did say he'd check in this morning to make sure I knew to expect his friend."

"Big of him. I take it you don't know the friend?"

"Heck, no. Ryan and I were an item in high school for about fifteen minutes before Cordelia got her claws into him. I know nothing about his college career, or his time in law school."

"A lawyer, huh? We might need one of those soon. Well, as long as his old pal doesn't expect much in the way of service, how much trouble could he be?"

"I have no idea. I hope I have some more clean sheets, and breakfast will be whatever I can find in the fridge."

"Beggars can't be choosers," Carroll said. "So, in addition to the coffee, I did find some English muffins and butter, so I guess the two of us are set." Carroll brought out all the goodies she'd found and laid them on the table, along with the coffeepot, and sat.

Of course that was when the phone rang, and of course it was Ryan. "Hey, Ryan," I said when I picked up.

"Good morning, Kate. Did you get my message last night?"

"Yes, lucky for you. We didn't get in until after ten. So you want to park your friend here?"

"Do you mind?"

"As long as he acknowledges that I haven't cleaned the house since I got here and there's not much food in the place — oh, and my friend Carroll from Philadelphia is staying here for a few days, and we won't be around much, then sure, he's more than welcome. When can he be here? Because we have to be somewhere else shortly. Oh, and does he know about you and me, back in high school?"

"Kate, I am a gentleman, so no. About Cordelia, he's had many an earful. As for your first question, we're parked outside."

I looked around at the messy kitchen — not Carroll's fault but mine — and my shabby clothes without a hint of chic, and said, "What the heck, come on in. At least there's coffee."

I stood up, pulled down my ratty T-shirt, and went to open the front door. They were already there. "Hey, Ryan, come on in. And this is?" I turned to get a good look at his friend, and then took another look. Taller than Ryan, aquiline features, hair just brushed with silver at the temples; casually dressed in impeccable jeans and what looked like extremely comfortable and expensive shoes suitable for trekking over battlefields. Damn, the man looked like he'd walked out of a magazine spread.

I was still gawking discreetly when the apparition extended his hand and said, "I'm Eric Harbison. You must be Kate."

"Welcome. Although I don't know why I should be the one to welcome you, because I'm just camping out here — the place actually belongs to Ryan, as he may have explained. We're not really open for business, but you're welcome to stay here, as long as you don't expect hotel-quality accommodations and service."

Eric smiled. Damn, his teeth were white. "Don't worry — Ryan explained the situation. He said you'd worked in the hotel industry until recently, and now you're trying to salvage this town? Is that a step up or a step down?"

"That remains to be seen. Oh, please, come in. My friend Carroll is in the kitchen — I asked her to come down for a few days and help catalog the papers left by the big man in town, circa 1900. Carroll's my go-to expert on historical documents. We plan to move the Barton collection to the town library once we know what we've got. Have you eaten?"

"We did," Ryan said, "but a cup of coffee would be great, and you can catch me up on what's been going on lately."

More than he would guess, I suspected.

# 14

We retreated to the kitchen and I filled coffee mugs all around. Then I went into hostess mode. "So, Eric, Ryan said you were in college together?"

"Yes. Mostly we hung out together, because our majors didn't overlap. But somehow we kept in touch after we graduated — it's all too easy to lose touch with your friends."

"Were you a history major? Ryan said in his message that you were doing a battlefield tour."

"Not at all — I was into business and finance. But after a few years of working I realized I'd missed a lot of things in this part of the country, so now I'm trying to catch up. You know — history, art, that kind of thing. I can't take a lot of time off, but I'm trying to make the most of it when I can. How about you? Ryan said you'd been working in Baltimore for quite a while."

"Yes. Great city, and I liked my job, but then a Japanese corporation bought the hotel out from under us. I feel bad for my boss, because he's got a couple of kids in college to support. I hadn't even begun to think about what I wanted to do next when my friend Lisbeth here in Asheboro called me and asked me to help save the town. How could I turn down something like that?"

"Sounds intriguing," Eric said. "I almost envy you. Do you have a plan?"

"Only a very preliminary one, and no money to support it yet. I don't suppose you have a spare couple of million dollars looking for a good cause?"

Eric smiled into his coffee cup. "Not exactly. Do you have fundraising experience?"

"Enough. Plus I've worked with construction crews and historic preservation groups in Baltimore, so I know who does what and how to get things done. You?"

"No. I manage money, but it's not mine. But I think I know what you mean — you see a lot of what goes on inside an organization, even if you're on the fringes in a different department."

"Exactly." I looked at Carroll. "You ready to get going?"

"You're leaving?" Ryan asked, looking disappointed.

"Yes. I told you we had to be somewhere. Carroll is cataloging the Barton letters at the mansion, and I'm hanging around nagging her to hurry up, so I know what I have to work with." I debated about telling him and his friend more about the project, but I was beginning to get nervous about saying too much about what we were doing to people I didn't know. I wasn't sure where Ryan fit in that spectrum and Eric was a wild card, so I wasn't ready to trust him. And with that murder . . . I needed to be cautious.

As if reading my mind, Eric said, "I thought I overheard someone mention that someone was killed in Asheboro?"

*Careful, Kate!* "Yes. On the fringes of town, actually. Nobody is sure why he was here in Asheboro, but he was definitely, uh, dead. The state police are investigating."

"Not local police?" Eric raised one eyebrow.

"Has Ryan driven you through town? The local police force consists of about ten people, including office staff. They pretty much confine themselves to traffic control and chasing down lost dogs, from what I've seen. There are no homicide investigators, so for anything more serious they call in the state police. I'm not criticizing them, but there's not enough serious crime here to justify spending money on a bigger department." Or at least there wasn't until I'd arrived.

"Do they know who the victim is?" Eric asked. It was a logical question, but one I didn't want to answer.

"I don't know. They haven't shared that information with me, and I'm not sure why they would. I happened to find the body, but I didn't know him." I hoped my lies were convincing.

"So he's not local?" Eric pressed.

"I haven't lived in this town for a long time, so I don't know who's local and who isn't." That at least was more or less true.

"What a shame. And I'm sorry it had to happen to you. Well, to get back to your project, I guess I haven't spent much time in small towns lately," Eric said, "but what you say sounds interesting, and may make economic sense. Don't let me keep you. Ryan and I may hang out for a while, but he tells me he's got to get to work too, so I'll take off and make the rounds looking at war memorials. I'm just happy he and I could get together."

"I can't say I've done that tour yet," I told

him, "except for a field trip to Gettysburg when I was in school here. I hope you enjoy it. Do you know how long you'll be staying?"

"I'm playing it by ear. It's kind of a treat, not having to stick to someone else's schedule. But don't worry about me — as long as I have a bed and coffee in the morning, I can look after myself."

"I'm glad to hear that," I told him. "I don't know when Carroll and I will be back. Ryan, you'll close up?"

"Sure. I've still got my keys. Uh, is there a bed made up?"

"I doubt it — I wasn't expecting company, beyond Carroll. But I'm sure you can figure things out. Good-bye, Eric — nice meeting you, and I assume I'll see you later. Oh, Ryan, be sure to give Eric a key *and* the code too."

We all stood up, and Carroll said, "I'll get my laptop and my notes. And my camera. Meet you at the car?"

"Fine."

While Carroll was upstairs I made a quick pass through the ground floor — mainly because I didn't trust Ryan to know enough to turn off a toaster. I smiled at the thought of him rummaging around all the closets in the house trying to find a set of sheets. I called out, "Bye, guys," as I went out the front door.

Carroll joined me a couple of minutes later. Once we were seated in the car, I said, "You were awfully quiet in there."

"Well, I did feel like a fifth wheel, since I know a bit about your history with Ryan. But I was trying to remember why Eric seemed familiar."

"Why would he? I did notice that he didn't mention where he lived or worked."

"I've got a lot of Philadelphia history stored in my head. He's a Harbison. You worked in the city for a while — does that ring any bells?"

"No, but I wasn't there all that long, and I wasn't into its history. What's important about his name?"

"Years ago — before your time — Harbison used to be a big name in dairy products in the greater Philadelphia area. But you know how any time someone is mentioned in the paper or on the news, there's always a little tagline? Like, 'John Smith, scion of the fondly remembered family that founded the Smith Widget Factory in the so-and-so neighborhood,' and so on."

"I remember hearing things like that, but what's it got to do with Ryan's buddy?"

"The Harbison dairy closed down before

I was born, but people still remember the giant milk bottle on top of what was the factory. I think it's a landmark now. If I remember correctly, Eric went into some other business, not the dairy."

"And this matters why?" I asked.

"It doesn't, really. But it seemed odd to me that he wouldn't mention anything about where he came from and where he works, especially since we all know Philadelphia."

"Maybe he thought we wouldn't be interested? Or he didn't want us to think he was trying to impress us?"

"Maybe. But doesn't he seem like a fish out of water in this little town of yours?"

"Maybe. But he's here as a tourist, to look at battlefields, or so he says. Guys like to do that, don't they? And he could work in a visit with old pal Ryan too."

We both fell silent for the last couple of miles to the mansion. I opened the gate, drove through, shut the gate — this was getting old! — and parked in front of the mansion. Josh's car was parked in its usual place in front of the carriage house.

When I turned off the engine, I asked Carroll, "Where do you want to start?"

"Where I left off, I guess. You want to help?"

"Gosh, and here I thought I wasn't qualified. Are you sure you trust me? What do I need to do?"

"Maybe some triage. Not all of the boxes in the attic are identified, so you could tag those with a short description, like 'carriage repairs.' If there's a removable cover, you could peek inside and see if there are any identifying features."

"I think I can handle that. Are you getting bored already?"

"No, just impatient. I want to get these records over to the library so I can take a serious look at them, under better conditions."

"Makes sense to me. Just point me in the right direction."

The sorting and tagging went quickly with two people working at it. I sympathized with Carroll's desire to get "intimate" with the files the day before, to get a feel for the man who wrote and collected and saved them all. But I had a different agenda: I wanted to get this phase done, to see if there was anything I could apply to my goal of remaking the town. I didn't downplay the importance of the original documents, but they'd be around for a while, and the town and I might not if I didn't get things moving forward soon. Playing with the documents was kind of self-indulgent on my part, since I should be talking to shop owners and checking the condition of the Main Street buildings, but on the other hand, it was something that could be accomplished in just a few days, and I really needed to finish at least one task.

By late afternoon Carroll and I were sitting at the bottom end of the attic stairs. We were sweaty, covered with dust, dirt, cobwebs, and maybe even some bat droppings — I hadn't looked too closely. Josh had not put in an appearance.

"Well," I said intelligently. Then stopped.

"That sums it up," Carroll said. Then she stopped.

Clearly we were tired. "What's your take on the collection as a whole, now that you've seen all of it?"

Carroll reflected. "Well, it has its merits. It's a lovely snapshot of life in a particular time and place." She didn't seem very enthusiastic.

"Is it something we could use at the town library, as an attraction? Or publish? Maybe Josh could help find a publisher. Of course, we wouldn't be pitching it as a scholarly tome," I ended dubiously.

"Tomes don't bring in much money,"

Carroll pointed out. "You might do better to turn it into historical fiction, or semi-fiction. You know, poor soldier survives the war, makes good, marries the love of his life, who then dies tragically in child-birth . . ."

"Hold on — we don't know whether there was or wasn't a child! Or one who died early. All we can say for sure is that there were no direct heirs mentioned in his will, which is why we're sitting here now."

"It doesn't matter, if it's fiction. It makes a better story. Then the grieving widower spends his remaining days wandering the empty halls of his sumptuous mansion, calling out his dead wife's name, and dies alone and forgotten."

"Are you volunteering to write this?" I asked as soon as I stopped giggling.

"No, but I could probably find someone who'd do it."

"Still doesn't help Asheboro much, unless it becomes a bestseller. How about poor Henry wandering the halls when he's struck by a brilliant idea and scribbles it down on a piece of paper and goes on to make the first automated widget in the country. *Then* he can die alone and forgotten, knowing that his widget will live on."

"It has possibilities," Carroll commented.

"Are we going back to town now, or do you want to check in with Josh first?"

"I'm not even sure where he is at the moment — he was going to meet Alison — and we aren't exactly working together. And he hasn't come looking for us." Was that a nonanswer?

"Remember that Eric Harbison will be staying at the B&B tonight, and who knows how long after that?"

My clothes looked worse than they had in the morning, no surprise. "How many battlefields are there? Maybe we should eat out somewhere. After we clean up a bit. Otherwise it'll be a drive-through window somewhere."

"To be honest, I really don't care right now. I want food and a shower, in any order you choose. Do you know if Eric is married?"

"Are you interested? Ryan didn't say, and I didn't notice a wedding ring, but that may not mean anything. You're going to have to find out for yourself." After about three seconds' consideration, I said, "Take-out food, then eat it at the B&B after we shower. Let Eric fend for himself if he wants to eat."

"Brilliant," Carroll replied.

So we picked up some nice greasy fast food and headed back to the B&B to get clean. Everything looked peaceful: a discreet number of lights were on inside, the front door was locked, and there were no cars except Carroll's parked behind the building. So I deduced that Ryan and Eric were off doing guy stuff singly or together, which was fine with me. Inside, Carroll and I split to our separate rooms, washed off the day's accumulated crud, then rendezvoused in the kitchen to eat. "Water? Lemonade? Wine?" I offered. "No beer, I'm afraid."

"I have heard wonderful hints about your wine cellar, and we don't have any other plans for the evening, so let's go with the wine."

"An excellent choice."

# 15

I managed to make it down the stairs before Carroll the next morning, and I started the coffee. After a few minutes I realized I hadn't heard any noise coming from Eric's room. But then, we'd left in such a hurry the day before that I wasn't even sure which room he'd chosen. I reminded myself that Eric wasn't my problem. Not that I expected Ryan to arrive and start scrambling eggs for him, but I knew I hadn't promised him breakfast.

Why was he here anyway? Based on his pedigree and his wardrobe, he could have stayed at any number of nice hotels in the region. Heck, he could have rented a house for a week or two. Why had Ryan offered him this place? It wasn't like he was going to make any money from Eric. Had he planted Eric here to keep an eye on me? But why would he do that?

The coffee was ready, so I poured myself

a cup, sat down at the kitchen table, and stared mindlessly into space. Carroll arrived a couple of minutes later, looking about the way I felt. "Good morning," I said.

Carroll blinked. "Is that coffee?"

"Yes. Help yourself. And I was joking. But I haven't heard a peep from Mr. Harbison. Maybe he's a heavy sleeper. Or maybe he didn't come home last night — I certainly didn't hear him, and I haven't looked for his car. Or maybe he's dead, but I'm not about to go up and check. Did you hear anything?"

Carroll shook her head slowly. "Not that I recall. That wine was outstanding, though. I think that's the last thing I remember."

"Consider it an inheritance from the late Cordelia. Best thing she ever did for me, apart from driving me out of town to seek my fortune."

Carroll did not respond to my feeble wit, and we sat silently until she had finished her first cup of coffee and looked more alive. "So, inventory round one accomplished," she finally said. "What now?"

"I arrange to get the collection moved to the library, at least temporarily."

"I'm going to assume that nothing's been changed at the library. Except they're done with that one bookcase there, and I'm pretty sure it was past saving. I hope your state police have a good cleanup crew."

"I think so. I should probably ask the mayor face-to-face about our movers, since we now know when we need them."

"Okay," Carroll agreed.

I went on, "And I should talk to some more of the townsfolk about my proposed town remodel. I've barely scratched the surface there. I think the pitch at the town meeting went over well, but people are going to want details, not just grand ideas."

"Do you have any? And why do you think you can make the town look like it did more than a century ago?"

"Because it still does, if you strip off the later additions. Ninety percent of the changes are purely cosmetic and will be easy to remove."

"Where are you putting the horses?"

I laughed. "Good question, Carroll. I need to do some research, but I'm going to guess any carriage houses weren't on Main Street but more likely on one of the parallel streets. I haven't even started looking at those yet. Do you think Henry would have had a car? Or a buggy with a driver?"

"I take it you haven't looked closely at the Barton carriage house? There could be some evidence, like oil stains on the floor, or maybe a lot of wrenches and automotive tools. And that apartment above that Josh is using would have worked for a chauffeur. But what I know about cars in that era would fill . . . well, not much of anything. As for whether Henry would have a car, as a prosperous factory owner — maybe you should ask Josh. That's closer to his area of expertise than to mine."

"I'll add that to my list of things to do. But I'd love to talk about any documentation you might know of regarding community development. Like, were there zoning changes in the beginning, or did people just build what they wanted? How did they allocate the costs for utilities? As a group, or store by store?"

"Kate, take a breath, will you? Let's go into town and go to the library and we can talk about how to lay out the Barton papers and where to store them, both short term and long term, if that's the way you all decide to go. Then you can give me the tour of the downtown district, or the parts I haven't seen. You keep telling me that the structural elements are still the original Victorian ones, but I want to see it for myself. Don't be insulted — I'm just being thorough. And trying to keep you under control."

I smiled. "You're my reality check — got it. So let's go. If Eric's here, he can fend for himself." I was a bit more concerned that I hadn't heard from Josh, since I wanted to touch base with him about a few things. If we were all really lucky, the Barton collection would have been moved to the library and be waiting eagerly for the attention of scholars by early next week. I hoped.

The way my luck had been running lately, I fully expected the library to have collapsed or fallen into a huge sinkhole since my last visit, so I was relieved when it appeared to be in the same state as I'd left it. "Nice building — Carnegie?" Carroll asked.

"I think so. That's easy to check."

"Must be a bear to retrofit for electronics."

"Frankly I don't think anyone's tried. I know the town hasn't had any money to throw at it."

"No county or state grants available?" Carroll asked.

"I'm not sure anyone has looked for them. I'll add that to the endless list. I hope that's the only problem, but I know that the, uh, former librarian made sure the place was physically sound. Electronics weren't her first priority."

"She was the one who was arrested, right?"

"Yes. But she's a good person. It'll be a while before she goes to trial, but I doubt she'll be coming back to Asheboro. The town is taking a 'wait and see' position before advertising the job, but the library will be closed while they wait."

I pulled into the parking lot and turned off my car, then dug out of my bag a set of keys to many of the Asheboro buildings. I'd forgotten to ask Detective Reynolds to return the set I'd given him, but he hadn't known I had extra sets. "You ready for this?"

"Of course. After two days working in that stuffy attic, this should be easy."

It felt odd to walk into the very silent library. The last time I'd been here . . . no, I didn't need to go there. I only wished that things had turned out in a different way. Of course Carroll didn't bring any of that baggage with her, and she was scanning the interior, calculating usable space. I could almost see her mind clicking through measurements. Me, I was worried about the security of the building. The builders and subsequent staff had been more concerned about keeping direct light off from the materials than thwarting thieves. "Will it work?" I asked.

"Is this all the space?" Carroll asked.

"The family history room is behind that door there — it has a big table, and that door locks."

"Good. I think we're going to need all of it, but only until we get things organized, not permanently. Oh, are there storage areas too?"

"I really can't tell you — they'd be in the basement, and I haven't been down there."

"I think we're good. Now we go talk to the mayor? What's his name?"

"Skip Bentley. He's not a world-beater but he's a good guy. He's a school principal, so his time is sort of flexible. I'm not sure he'll be in today, but he might be, if there's some town business to take care of. We'll find out."

"Is the town council a rowdy bunch?"

"No, not really. I think they're kind of burned out these days, what with all the financial crises, and Cordelia's death didn't make things any better. They're glad she's gone, because she was something of a pain in the butt, but the underlying problems are still there. Let's walk over to the town hall and I can introduce you to whatever staff is around. If Skip's not in, I can leave him a note or a message and tell him what we need, but he should be expecting it. Anyway, you can get a sense of the town along the way."

"Lead on!" Carroll seemed to be getting into the spirit of my vision, which was a plus. I definitely needed cheerleaders, both for my own state of mind and to help me convince the rest of the town that I was not crazy.

Skip was not in his office, no surprise, but I chatted with his assistant, Beverly, for a while.

"I was so sorry to hear about what happened at the library, Kate. Do the police know anything more?" Beverly asked.

"Not that they've told me." When I explained what my errand was, she snorted. "Hey, he's already handed that little task over to me anyway. How many people do you think you need?"

I turned to Carroll. "You'd know better than I would. I'd guess we want to get it done fairly quickly, because people have a lot of other things they'd like to do with their free time."

Carroll said quickly, "The ideal crew would be four strong men in their twenties. Can you recruit a team like that, Beverly?"

"Since it's not sports season, no problem. You want them today?"

"Tomorrow would probably be better," I

told Beverly. "We can wait for them at the library. Oh, and they'll need a truck or two."

"Of course," Beverly said. "I've got your cell number — I'll give you a call when the guys are ready to roll."

"Beverly, you are a miracle worker. While I have your attention, do you have any ideas about what you'd like to see in the new old town?"

"Sure do — a lady's hat shop. I'm always sorry that women stopped wearing the fancy ones, but I guess those society ladies had to spend more time fussing with them than getting anything else done. Maybe that was the point."

"I love the idea. Assuming, of course, we can find anybody who knows how to make that kind of hat. And decorations that don't wipe out entire populations of endangered species. I seem to recall that hatmakers used to put dead birds on some of them."

"Can't imagine wearing a dead bird on my head," Beverly said. "You know about the straw factory?"

I shook my head. "Never heard of it. What did they do?"

"Wove straw into the stuff that the hats were made of. Went out of business in the 1890s when hat styles changed."

"How on earth do you know this?"

"My great-grandmother worked there before she got married. Bet I've got some pictures of her at home."

"I love it! Please share!" I said, delighted. How many other people in town had family stories to tell?

"Got another idea, while you're asking. How about you run a contest or something in the paper, asking for other ideas? You could give away some sort of prize, maybe, but I bet it would make the people who read the paper feel a little more connected to the town and the project."

"That's brilliant! What's the paper like these days?"

"It's weekly, and strictly local, but that's what you need. And they've got a lot of old files."

"Tell me who I should talk to and I'll get in touch with him."

"Her." When I looked confused, she said, "Editor's a woman. Frances Carter. She's been running it forever."

"That's great." Although if I was going to think about re-creating the paper from back then, I had doubts about how many small-town women editors there might have been before 1900. "Look, we'll grab a bite to eat and then hang around the library waiting for a bit — please let me know if your crew will be coming tomorrow. Thanks so much for your help!"

"Happy to be useful. Just don't let the mayor grab all the credit for it."

"Got it. But I am happy to share the spotlight if it helps."

Back on the street I turned to Carroll. "Hungry yet? Not that there are many choices within walking distance."

"That'll have to change, whether or not it's historically accurate."

"I was thinking of a tearoom," I said a bit defensively. "I figured most of the men were working, but women might have wanted to have a cup of tea after their arduous afternoon of picking out new hats. The farmers probably didn't come into town at all, male or female, unless it was for something practical like cattle feed. Patrons of food establishments would have to have some disposable income for their tea and scones or whatever they ate. Which dovetails with the surge of industrial activity in the area."

"By George, I think you've got the hang of this," Carroll said, grinning. "But you've still got a lot of work to do. Like, how do you assign space, both in size and location? I would guess that a grocer would need a larger shop than a shoemaker. And what would you do about someone who has diversified and has to make as much use of his space as possible, even if what he's selling is nothing more than a hodgepodge of stuff that caught his eye? I saw a citation somewhere about a stationer in Lynn who opened a small art gallery at the back of the store, which I think did well."

"Harder to promote, I'd guess, but interesting, as long as the owner doesn't try to go in too many directions. But I can see a link from writing paper to art supplies to artists."

"Exactly. Look, we should eat, so we're ready when and if your friend Beverly calls. Forget history — let's just find edible food."

We found a place halfway down the block. I didn't remember it from my earlier days, or if I did, it was something like a phone store or a repair shop. Little had been done to improve the interior, unless the dust of ages past was considered a contemporary fashion statement. Back outside after our meal, we stood on the sidewalk, uncertain. I checked my phone to see if it was on and charged. Yes to both, but no calls or messages.

"What now?" Carroll asked.

"I don't know. I don't want to start talking to someone in town here and then be called away. I doubt our big move will happen today, but if it does, I should stay here at the library to direct whoever does the heavy lifting. You can go out to the mansion and supervise the removal? That way we can be sure that people are careful at both ends."

"Makes sense. Unless it gets to be too late in the day — the light in the attic is lousy."

"Good point. We'll just have to wait and see for a while."

"What else have you got in mind for the town?" Carroll asked.

"I'd love to find an old map, or even a town directory, for Asheboro. Maybe you could help with that?"

"Sure, no problem. What about the factory? When are we going to see that?"

"Down at the far end of town. As for when, let's see how the rest of the cataloging goes."

"Hmm," Carroll said, almost to herself. "You said there was no train line here, so whatever came in or went out would have had to be delivered by carriage. Which means there would be some size and weight limitations."

"Do you know, I never thought about that? I guess shovels could be divided into manageable parcels. Do you know what would be needed to make the metal parts? Or would they have been made somewhere else and delivered here to be assembled?"

"I'd go with the first idea, but you should ask Josh — he's the expert on manufacturing in that period."

"I had the impression that he was more interested in the sociological and social aspects than the details of how things got done."

"If you ask me, for a historian that's cheating. You need to know the nuts and bolts of a process before you can examine how it fit within a community or a region. You know, all those messy details about shipping and forging and storing and stuff."

"And that's exactly why I called for help — you. You and Josh need to sit down and talk about it, and then tell me what I need to know. I don't want to look like an idiot because I forgot to consider where supplies would come from and where they would be stored."

"How much longer will Josh be around?"

"Till the end of summer, I think."

"Then pump him for all the information you can, or at least where to find it."

"I'll put that at the top of the list."

# 16

Carroll and I ambled through the center of town, but the choices for lunch were limited, and I wasn't in the mood for fast food. "You know," I said, "there's a soda shop along here, that's been here since I was a kid. We can get something to eat there and finish our survey of the town."

"I'm game," Carroll said.

I found the place, and we sat at a table and ordered iced teas and hamburgers. While we waited, I studied the place. It wouldn't fit my Victorian model, but it still suggested what had been a small town where everyone knew each other to chat with, that was relatively clean, with low crime.

I looked up to see the owner, Ted, delivering our plates. He was smiling at me. "You're Ted, right?" I asked.

"Sure am. You used to come in, back in

the day. I remember your face, but not your name."

"I'm Kate Hamilton. Yes, my folks used to live in town, but they moved a few years ago. And this is my friend Carroll, who's never been to Asheboro before. Ted, I'd love to talk to you about the changes in Asheboro, but I think I'd have to come back for that," I said.

"Anytime you like, young lady. I'm always here."

"Next week, then, I hope."

When Ted had walked away, I checked my phone again: no calls or messages from Beverly or anyone else.

Beverly didn't call until late Saturday afternoon, and said we could plan to move on Sunday. By then Carroll and I had checked out the entire town center (not that it took long, given there were only four full blocks of it) and scribbled a lot of ideas on scraps of paper, so our time wasn't wasted. No way could we use all of the ideas, but at least we had choices, and I really appreciated having a second set of eyes thanks to Carroll.

Toward the end of our stroll I realized that I recognized one of the stores from my childhood. It was fairly large, with a surprisingly high ceiling, although it was only one story high. Currently it appeared to be an odd mishmash of a hardware store, which was clearly not its intended use, but some of the shelving appeared to be original, and I really wanted to know what lay under the dingy tiles that covered the ceiling. When we walked in, and I stopped and almost sniffed the air: it *felt* old, despite the modern additions.

"Hello?" I called out.

"Coming, coming . . . ," a man's voice called out from the back of the store somewhere. It took him at least two minutes to appear, shuffling his feet along the worn floorboards. "What can I help you lovely ladies with?" he asked.

I didn't answer immediately because the man looked familiar, and I was running through my mental database trying to place him. "Mr., uh, MacDonald?"

The man's bright eyes focused on me, and I saw a spark of recognition. "You're the Hamilton girl, aren't you?"

"Not a girl anymore, but yes, I'm Kate Hamilton. I'm amazed you remember me."

"Never were that many people coming into the store, so it wasn't that hard. Your mother used to stop by now and then. How's she doing?"

"She and my dad moved to Florida a

couple of years ago. They love it there. So you still own this place?"

"Paid off the mortgage years ago. Sitting here is better than sittin' at home watching that damn boob tube."

I had to suppress a smile: I hadn't heard a television called that for a long time. "Good for you!"

"So, what brings you back to town? I don't suppose you're looking for nails."

"No, not right now. Tell me, do you go to town meetings?"

Mr. MacDonald shook his head. "Nah, damn waste of time. And I don't see too good to drive at night anymore. My son goes, though."

"He doesn't work with you?"

"He's with one of those big construction companies just outside Baltimore. Still lives in town here, though."

I made a mental note: a construction contact who knew the history of the town could be useful, if we ever got this project off the ground. "Have you heard about the project to turn this town back into a Victorian village?"

"Now why would you want to do a damn fool thing like that?"

"To bring in tourists — and money."

"Ah. Town's really managed to screw up

the money side of things. So you want to tart it up, make it look old-fashioned?"

I laughed. "Well, yes, if you put it that way. But I have to say, this place could pretty much pass as Victorian just as it is. You just need to peel off some of the later additions. Like the ceiling tiles. You know what's under them?"

"Whatever they used when the place was built. That sort of pressed tin stuff."

My heart leaped. This was the first tangible proof that the old materials were still there under the modern ones. Assuming Mr. MacDonald remembered correctly. "Has this always been a hardware store?"

"Sure thing. I took over from my dad, some sixty years ago. It had sat empty for a while, so he got it for a good price during the Depression, but it was a hardware store even before that. And we're still here, except my son doesn't want anything to do with the place. Says it's old-fashioned."

"It is, but that could be a good thing. Do you remember other things about the town, back when you were a kid?"

"Sure do. School was down the road a ways, and I walked from there to here when our day was over. I knew everybody along the way, and their kids."

I wanted to hug him. A firsthand account

of the way things used to be in Asheboro was worth as much to me as a library filled with old advertising flyers. "Mr. MacDonald, can I come by and talk to you sometime soon? For more than just a few minutes? I'd love to hear more about Asheboro back then."

"Sure thing. I'm always here, 'cept on Sundays. So you're gonna stick around for a while?"

"Looks like it. Thank you so much — it's been a pleasure meeting you again."

Once outside I couldn't stop grinning. This whole project was a crazy seesaw — up one minute, down the next. I believed in the concept of a restored village, but I wasn't so sure I could sell it. Still, having pieces of the "real" story from people like Mr. MacDonald made my case so much more appealing.

"You really got lucky with that man," Carroll said. "And with Ted. I'm beginning to believe this could work."

"I'm very happy to hear you say that!"

"I mean it." Carroll laughed. "But you've got a lot of work to do. You given any thought to modern code restrictions?"

I stopped in my tracks on the sidewalk. "Are you trying to be a buzzkill?"

"No, just being realistic," Carroll countered.

"Duly noted. But can I please be happy for just a little while?"

"Of course. Dreams are cheap. But can I ask you something?"

"Sure," I told her.

"Is this just a project for you, to keep you busy while you figure out what to do next with your life? Or do you really care about this town? Are you going to see it through? Stick around to help manage it, if does get built?"

I couldn't answer that. "To be honest, Carroll, I don't know yet. I love the concept, but it's been only a few weeks, and we're still in the talking stages. Ask me in a couple of months. In the meantime, is there anything else we should do about the Barton papers today?"

"We know the library's set to go. What time is the moving crew supposed to arrive at the mansion?"

"Nine, I think. How long do you think it will take to shift the stuff?"

"Depends on how many guys and how big a truck. We should be done by noon, I hope."

"Then what?"

"I disappear into the library after they

unload and figure out what we've got. And don't ask me how long that will take because I don't have a clue."

"You want Josh to help?"

"Up to him. I don't know how this small-town stuff will play into what he's working on, but surely he's gotten a boost for finding the Clara letters."

I shrugged. "Maybe — I'm not plugged into the academic community. But I think he may be more interested than he was at the start."

"I wonder if Alison will still be around. Because I think the three of us — you and me plus Josh — are more than enough to get started on the papers. Four would just complicate matters, especially if she doesn't have any experience with old documents."

Carroll fell silent, then she perked up. "Do we have time to look at the factory once we get done with the library?"

"Oh, right, we were going to explore that next. I thought you wanted to go through the documents from the house first?"

"Yes and no," Carroll said. "For one thing, we don't know if there is anything useful at the factory. For another, even if there is, it may not be relevant. If anything does exist, and it does prove to be relevant, then I'd like to look at all the papers as a whole, alongside Henry's personal life. We won't know until we look."

"Apparently I have infected you with this bug. But I'll admit what you suggest makes sense. Then we only have to go through everything one time. Today or tomorrow?"

"I think it's getting kind of late to start on the factory now. Let's see what kind of time we have left tomorrow after we move the stuff. Otherwise we can start early on Monday. You said you'd never been inside the factory?"

"That's right. I might have known some kids who checked it out, but their interests were anything but historical. It's a wonder somebody didn't burn the building down. I'm going to take a wild guess that the place is pretty much stripped bare, so there shouldn't be many places to look."

"Damn, I wish I'd brought more grubby clothes. I wasn't expecting to go climbing through abandoned buildings."

"Don't worry — there's a washer at the B&B. We might as well go back there anyway."

When we arrived, Eric Harbison's car was in the driveway and Josh's was parked at the curb, along with Ryan's. Apparently any private conversations were out of the question for the evening. I opened the door and called out, "Hello? Anybody home?"

"In the front parlor," Josh called out.

I led Carroll to the room to find the three men — Josh, Eric, and Ryan — looking very relaxed as they reclined in substantial plush-upholstered mahogany chairs. The half-empty glasses of wine in their hands might have played a role in that.

"Welcome, ladies. Can we offer you something to drink?" Ryan asked.

I glanced at Carroll, and she shrugged. Apparently she had made the same deduction as I had: we'd have to talk later. "Why not? That is, if you've left anything for us."

"There is an ample supply, I assure you." Josh said. At least I thought that was what he had said — he seemed to have mislaid a number of consonants, but he appeared to be enjoying himself. He managed to fill glasses for Carroll and me without spilling, at least.

"I'm glad to hear that. So, what have you all been up to this afternoon?" I asked, as I settled in another of the chairs.

Eric spoke first. "Ryan was kind enough to show me the lay of the land around here. Beautiful country. So sad that it was sullied by the horrors of battle." He too sounded a bit over the top.

"I've been filling them in on the sad life of Henry Barton," Josh said.

"Including the Barton letters?" Carroll asked.

"Of course. It's a charming story."

"I've lined up some people to help us transfer the papers from the mansion's attic to the library tomorrow," I told them. "It should take most of the day. And before you volunteer, I think that's enough people."

I shot a warning glance at Carroll. I wasn't sure what interest either Ryan or Eric Harbison might have in stacks of old documents, but I thought I'd play it safe and keep my cards close to my vest. Let them think we'd be tied up all day, and the letters wouldn't be left unguarded.

Why did that word come to mind? Didn't I trust these people? In a word, no. Zach Mitchell was dead, and there was still no explanation for his death.

"Did you have plans for dinner?" I hoped no one thought I was volunteering to cook.

To my relief, Ryan spoke up quickly. "I wanted to show Eric this great restaurant in Bethesda. Hope you don't mind."

"Of course not," I told him. "Carroll and I have had a long day, and tomorrow will be even longer, I'll bet. You boys go ahead and have fun. Eric, you have your key, right?"

"I do. I'll let myself in when I get back, and I'll try not to make too much noise." He stood up. "Ready, Ryan?"

"As ever I'll be," Ryan said, wobbling a bit. "Ladies, nice to see you again."

I made good-bye noises and watched as they made their unsteady way out the front door. I hoped they were safe to drive. Josh hadn't gone with them, so I asked, "What was that all about?"

"Two old buddies having a chat? Plus me."

"Along with a bottle or two of good wine." Well, technically it was Ryan's wine, so he had every right to enjoy it. "And when did you come in?"

"I was looking for you. I thought you might be finished by now."

"Did Alison leave?"

"I think so. We shared what information we had, and if I come up with any other ideas, I can email her. How'd your day go?"

I topped off my wineglass. "Carroll had created order out of chaos in the attic. Then we prepped the library to receive all the stuff. Then we stopped by the town hall and arranged for people to move it all tomorrow. Then we had lunch at Ted's café — he's been here forever — followed by a nice chat with a guy in town who I remember from my early days here — he has a wonderful old hardware store in town that was his father's before it was his. And that about sums up our day. How about you?"

Josh sighed. "I wish I had accomplished half of what you two did."

"Well, tomorrow is another day."

# 17

Since we had no guests at the B&B and Carroll and I were exhausted, we decided to send Josh to hunt for pizza, which gave Carroll and me a short while to confer about our plans.

"So we're good to go?" I asked.

"I hope so," Carroll said dubiously. "I always worry when people who aren't trained in handling fragile old documents toss them around, but I'll try to keep an eye on them. Same at your end. Don't let them sling bundles of stuff around. I'd better sketch out what I think should go where in the library, but the labeling on the boxes isn't always clear. It's going to be a complicated day."

"I believe it. We'll just have to do the best we can."

"Hey, I forgot to tell you: I found some documents about the renovations to the mansion — wouldn't you just love to see an invoice from the Tiffany studios? — although I'd guess the deeds and such would be held at the bank or a law firm. And wills, but I assume that various attorneys have combed through those in the past, so I wouldn't expect any surprises there. I wonder if you might find invoices for materials and supplies that Henry ordered for the property, but I didn't happen to see anything referring to the factory. Which does not mean there aren't any documents for that, only that I didn't find them. You can do some further sorting once the stuff gets to the library. Maybe put all the family records and correspondence in the family history room, and segregate the house-related items on one table in the main room. Use your judgment. It's not an overwhelming amount of material. Are we supposed to be paying the moving crew?"

"Actually, I don't know. I need to talk to Ryan again about setting up a nonprofit organization for this whole thing, if he thinks that's appropriate. If he can't do it, maybe he can recommend someone who can. And I'll keep track of expenses. I guess I should make up a handout — people should know that they can claim any out-of-pocket costs as tax deductible, but I should probably keep my eye on those in case anybody tries to stiff us." I figured I probably had enough in savings to cover the early stages, thanks to my severance package — but not for long.

"Have you decided what you want to do with the Barton papers, after they're cataloged?" Carroll asked.

"Not really. I don't suppose the library is appropriate. I'd rather see it remain open to the community — assuming the town finds a librarian — rather than house a small private collection with limited access. But I'm not sure what our other options are. I'd certainly like to keep the papers in Asheboro, assuming they're more than just a jumble. Maybe Josh has some ideas."

"You could carve out a space in the factory, if that makes sense."

"I suppose. But that's one more big thing I haven't had time to think about. Maybe it might fall down any minute — we'd need a good structural engineer to tell us, and of course, that would mean spending more money. Maybe there's nothing to be done with the place, and the town might as well tear it down because it's a safety risk. Right now it's just an empty shell."

"Well, you said you liked challenges," Carroll pointed out. "And if it's empty, you can do whatever you want with it, if it's structurally sound. It was the principal business in the town circa 1900, and also the commercial counterpart to the mansion."

"Good points, Carroll. I'm glad you're here to throw ideas at me. Now if only I could clone myself, I might actually get something done."

At that point Josh came in with two pizza boxes, so talking stopped. We gorged ourselves, then tossed the trash. "Thanks, Josh. You going to help out tomorrow?"

"I guess, as long as I don't have to do the heavy lifting," he responded with little enthusiasm.

"What, getting old? I'll be at the library laying things out. That may be more your speed."

"Deal. I'd better get back to my place. See you in the morning."

When Josh had left I turned to Carroll. "Bed?"

"Sounds like a plan. Give me a key to the mansion and your gate code, and I'll head out there whenever I get up. What time are you aiming to be at the library?"

"Eight, maybe? I'll make one more pass through, and maybe label some of the spaces to help our moving crew, in case any of the papers are actually identified. But I don't expect too much."

"I hate to be ghoulish, but do you think the volunteers will know that a man died there this week?" Carroll asked. "And are they going to ask inconvenient questions?"

"I . . . really don't know. What can we tell them, anyway? We know his name, and that he was a student. We do not know why he was in Asheboro or why he was inside the library. We certainly don't know who killed him, and I'm pretty sure the public still thinks it was an accident. So all we can answer is 'I don't know.' "

"True. I'll give you a call tomorrow whenever I'm ready to shut things down at the mansion. Or you can call my cell if something comes up."

"I'm hoping at least one thing will go right. Don't forget to lock up when you're done at the mansion!"

"Right, chief. I'll meet you at the library, or if you're not there, I'll come back here to the B&B."

"Sounds like a plan," I said.

Carroll headed up the stairs while I went around checking that all the doors and windows were locked tight. I didn't know if it made a difference, but it made me feel better.

I didn't hear Eric come in before I fell asleep.

■ ■ ■ ■

Carroll was long gone by the time I meandered downstairs in the morning, so I allowed myself one cup of coffee and another stale muffin before setting out for the library.

Maybe this was all a useless exercise. We'd gotten spoiled by finding Clara's letters first, based on somebody else's hunch, but there was no guarantee there would be anything of interest in the rest of the documents. But at least we could check that off our list of things to do. Quite possibly the factory building would prove equally barren, and then we could move on. I still had most of the merchants in the village to talk to, and while I'd been lucky so far, there were bound to be naysayers who would bail out on my grand scheme. I wasn't sure if the town had the money to buy them out at the moment — or maybe ever. That wouldn't make the merchants happy, but it might give them some small incentive to stick around and see how things worked out, as long as they went along with the plan. Could the town seize their properties through eminent domain? That wouldn't make *anybody* happy. I didn't dare think of any renovations that would be needed to fit my vision, much less of where the money for those would come from.

Dressed in comfortable — and washable — clothes, I set out for the library just after eight. Eric's car was parked outside the B&B, but I still hadn't heard a peep from him. Either the man slept a lot, or he was hiding from Carroll and me. I reminded myself once again that he and his creature comforts were not my problem. I had a document collection to welcome.

While waiting for the first delivery (*out of how many?* I wondered), I strolled around the silent library. It seemed frozen in time, but not in a good way, or one that would be useful to me. It was simply kind of sad. I knew the former librarian, Audrey, had done her best, but she'd had little money from the town to work with, and so many people had been diverted by electronic devices of their own that they had all but forgotten there was a library. It was a modestly handsome building, and the period was right for my projected remodel of the town, but was there a better way to use the space? A place to kill someone was not on the short list. Poor Audrey — she would have been horrified at what had happened in "her" library.

The first van pulled up after an hour or so, manned by a quartet of brawny high school kids who looked like they were football players, and I played traffic director and told them where to set down their loads. They made quick work of it and left to collect their next batch. A second van pulled up just as they were leaving, and we repeated the process. I kept an eagle eye on the piles of boxes, hoping there was enough space in the library to lay them all out, but I had no idea how much more was coming.

Josh appeared around ten. "Wow, I had no idea there was this much in the attic."

"If there had been less, you would have missed all the fun," I said, trying not to sound too sarcastic. "The attic was bigger, so the piles looked smaller. No, guys, over at that end!" I called out and waved at the helpers who were heading in the wrong direction with their loads. Then I turned back to Josh. "Everything okay back at the mansion?"

"Carroll has it under control," Josh said. "And it's going fast. Where do you want me?"

"Can you keep an eye on the family history room? That's closer to your area of expertise. If you find something that doesn't belong, just set it aside for now and we'll sort things out later."

"Yes, ma'am." Josh headed for the large room at the back, where the big work table seemed half-filled already. I wasn't surprised to see him sit down and start reading a page.

Two more van loads and the guys told me that the job was finished. I was happily surprised. Carroll had guessed right; it wasn't quite noon. I called her on my cell.

"You're done?" I said.

"Looks like it."

"No surprises?"

"Nope. Just a lot of dirt. And a lost hat pin. How's your end?"

"Not bad. There's still some room left. I put Josh to work on the stuff in the family history room, and he promptly got side-tracked. At least he wasn't in the way. Are you headed here next?"

"I think so — after I lock up, of course. Want me to pick up some food?"

"One should never bring food or drink into a library," I said in a mock-prim voice.

Carroll made an obnoxious noise. "How about fast food and we eat it on the bench out front?"

"Works for me. Get enough for Josh, will you? If he doesn't want it, we can finish it later."

“Deal. See you in maybe half an hour.” Carroll hung up.

# 18

When I went back inside, Josh was still engrossed in some pages he'd pulled out in the family history room. "We've got the whole lot here now," I told him. "You found something interesting?"

It took him a moment to focus on the here and now. "What? Oh. Maybe. Is the moving done?"

"Yes, sir — the football team took care of it while you were reading in here. Carroll's on her way back from the mansion, and she'll pick up some food."

"Great," he said absently. "Look, you think there's any way we can check out the factory this afternoon?"

"What? Transferring the whole collection in a few hours isn't enough work for one day?"

"I may have found something. But I don't want to say much until I've checked it out — I don't want to get your hopes up. It shouldn't take long to check."

"Great. So now you want to dig around in the factory building, which is no doubt filthy and has neither air-conditioning nor light. Sounds like fun."

"I thought you wanted to know where Henry's bankroll came from," Josh demanded.

Clearly he was dangling a carrot in front of me. "Carroll and I were talking before you showed up, and we figured the odds were slim that there was anything worthwhile in the building there. You think we should check anyway?"

"Yes, I do. Come on, it probably won't take long. You can stay here and help Carroll if you'd rather. Just lend me the keys."

Why was he suddenly being secretive? I had thought we were all in this together. Well, if he didn't want to talk, I wasn't about to offer him any of my greasy lunch.

I was startled to hear an unfamiliar female voice call out from the front of the building. "Hello? Anybody here?"

I must have left the door unlocked, so I went quickly to greet the unexpected visitor. It had to be Alison. I made a quick assessment: blond, about my age, or a little older; nicely but casually dressed and wearing comfortable shoes. She wasn't exactly petite, and she looked sturdy — and shapely, I admitted grudgingly. She appeared to be more interested in looking around the building than looking at me.

To my surprise, Josh had followed me. "Hi, Alison," he said. "I didn't expect to see you."

"I thought I might as well see what's available here in the library, while I'm in the area. And I saw there were some people in here." She finally looked at me, then extended a hand. "You must be Kate Hamilton. I'm sorry we didn't get a chance to talk. Josh told me about your proposed project. I love the concept of what you're trying to do in this town — very ambitious."

"I'm finding that out. It's nice to meet you at last, but I guess we've both been busy. Are you an academic too?"

"I had hoped to be when I was in college, but somehow I ended up in the corporate world. But I still dabble in aspects of industrial history, as Josh knows. He said you were moving all the documents from the mansion attic to this building?"

"We just finished that. Did Josh tell you about the Clara Barton papers?"

"He did. What a delight, to find a piece of history that way. Just waiting to be discovered."

"We were very lucky. I'm hoping we'll find something more in this mass of material." I waved vaguely at the boxes and piles of papers on all the horizontal surfaces in sight.

"Didn't Josh tell me you grew up in this town?" Alison asked as she wandered among the tables reading labels on the boxes.

"I did, but I left and never looked back until recently."

"Has the town changed much?"

"Yes and no. The underlying structures are still here, and the modern changes are mostly superficial. The town as a whole has kind of dwindled. Did you and Josh get to cover what you needed?"

Alison glanced at Josh. "This was mainly an exploratory trip. He may have told you that I've been asked to give a presentation at a conference in Wilmington in the fall, and I thought it would be more efficient to ask an expert — that would be Josh — than to start doing the research from scratch."

At that moment Carroll returned with our impromptu lunch. She pulled up in front of the building and parked, and I went out to greet her.

"The mysterious Alison has appeared," I told her. "She's inside talking to Josh."

"Interesting. I thought she was on her way out of town."

"Apparently she decided to check out the library before she left. You have enough food for all of us?"

"I think so. Will she be staying?"

"I don't know. Listen, before she showed up Josh told me he's on the trail of something he thinks is important, and he wants to check out the factory to see if there are any records there."

"Isn't that what we've been saying all along?" Carroll demanded.

"Yes, but he thinks he's found other hints, not that he's shared them. I don't know how much he's told Alison, and he's been pretty secretive, so let's not mention the factory in front of Alison. Or let Josh take the lead, if he wants."

"Got it. Let's eat!"

Inside the library I introduced Alison and Carroll, and we went back outside to eat — there was no table space left, and I didn't want to get grease on antique documents. I'd forgotten how quiet Sundays were in this town. We hadn't seen a single person pass by on the sidewalk, and surprisingly few cars. It took us no more than fifteen minutes to eat, and collect and toss our trash.

Alison was the first to leave. "I'd better head home; I've got to be at work in the morning. Thank you for all your help, Josh. May I call or email you if I have any more questions?"

"Sure, no problem," he told her.

Then she turned to Carroll and me. "Good luck with your project. I look forward to seeing what you make of this place."

"Keep your fingers crossed for us. And if your company wants to make a nice donation, we'll put the name on something. You want a building? A park?"

Alison laughed. "One step at a time! But I'll keep in touch." She turned toward what must have been her car, while Carroll, Josh, and I went back into the library for one last view.

"What's the security here?" Carroll asked nervously while we waited for Josh to finish his perusal.

"Latches on the windows, and dead bolts on the front and back doors. No fancy electronics. Pathetic, I know," I told her. Smashing a window was all too easy, as we had found out. "I'd better ask the town to keep the lights on in here, so anybody rummaging around would be obvious from the outside. Maybe get brighter lightbulbs."

"Could be I'm overreacting," Carroll said. "I'm used to working in museum or big library settings, where there really is valuable stuff worth taking. Here, I'm not sure a passing citizen would recognize a valuable document unless it said, 'George Washington Signed This!' in big red letters. No offense meant — it's a different standard."

"I know, I get it. But the whole blinking town knows what we've been doing today. I'm sure Beverly called plenty of people to find enough to help us out. At least it's on the main street, so anybody poking around inside, with or without a flashlight, would be obvious. And maybe now the mansion will be safe, since all the documents are here."

Carroll sighed. "I hate to have to remind you, Kate, but somebody died here just days ago. The mansion may be in the clear, but I don't think I feel entirely safe here, or not alone, anyway." When I started to protest, she raised a hand. "I know, I know," Carroll said. "I'm probably worrying for nothing."

"No, you're right. The only reason the man died that makes sense to me is that there is something that someone thinks is valuable somewhere in the collections, and the killer thought it was worth killing for."

"We're going to the factory now, right?" Josh asked.

"Is it really that important to you?" I said to him.

"Sorry, I don't mean to be mysterious, but as a good academic I want to be sure of my hypothesis before I start spreading it around. I'd hate to look foolish if I'm wrong. So the sooner I find what is — or isn't — there, the sooner I can confirm my guesses. As far as I can tell, the Barton Shovel Factory is the last possible place to look. So, what can you tell me about the Barton Shovel Factory? I mean from your own recollections?"

This whole business of the documents was beginning to drive me crazy. "Not a lot. You probably know as much as I do about it, or maybe more. In case you can't remember, kids aren't usually interested in shabby old factory buildings. Or at least, not female kids. The place was closed down by the time I was old enough to notice it, and in theory nobody was allowed inside. It didn't look sufficiently spooky to go poking around on Halloween, and it was on the fringes of town, with not much else around it. I've been told it employed a lot of people in its heyday, but that was quite a while ago. What do you think you're looking for?"

"Legal documents. I'll know it when I see it," he replied cryptically. "You two up for walking?"

"Sure. I think we both need to stretch a

bit. So, answer my question."

Instead of giving me a direct answer, Josh took off on a tangent. "How much do you know about the history of electric lighting?"

"Not much. Why?" He proceeded to tell me all about it. We were walking along the nearly empty street, the Barton factory looming ever larger at the far end. While Josh was in lecture mode, Carroll hung back, admiring the buildings at this far end of town. The factory took up the greatest space, but apart from size it wasn't very impressive. It was a very plain, very blocky brick building, with only a few arched windows to break up its plainness. Four stories high, with some rickety wooden shutters on the uppermost two stories and a regularly spaced row of chimneys emerging from the top of the building. It was only when you saw a human walking by at street level that you realized how large the individual windows were. The building was larger than it looked.

Josh began speaking again. "I think there's evidence that Henry made more than shovels in the building, but I can't prove it yet. And he might not have been thinking of selling his product. I think he was bored and used his ample spare time to tinker with things. Then the death of his wife threw him into a depression from which he never recovered, and he lost interest in what he'd been working on. If that's true, then the evidence may be stashed somewhere in the building. We know it wasn't at his house."

"Are you going to give us a hint of what we're looking for?" I asked.

"Not yet. But it may include diagrams."

"Why are you being so cryptic? It would help if we all knew what we were looking for."

"Kate, we don't even know if there *are* any documents in the building, much less relevant ones. This is a long shot."

I studied Josh's expression for a moment and decided that whatever this was, he believed that it was real and it was important. "Then let's go hunting."

# 19

Josh seemed impatient to get into the factory building, so he picked up his pace, and Carroll and I followed. I hung back slightly and waited for Carroll to catch up.

"What was that all about?" she asked in a low voice.

"Josh thinks — or at least hopes — that there's something important hidden somewhere in the building, but he won't tell me what it is. I guess that's his male ego — he doesn't want to appear stupid if there's nothing to be found. But we said we'd look, right? Might as well follow through, and we can regroup when we're finished."

"You've never been in the building?"

"Nope. Never even tried. It may be that braver souls than I tried and found nothing of interest, and somehow that word got passed around. Nice building, though, isn't it?"

"Basic Victorian brick — 1880s?" Carroll

said, clearly not impressed.

"I'm no expert, but that sounds about right."

"You've got the key, so nobody's going to arrest us for breaking and entering, right?"

"As far as I know. I was entrusted with all the keys to the municipal parts of the town, so I suppose I'm allowed. Nobody said I couldn't bring guests."

Josh was already standing by the arched main door, all but twitching with excitement. "Come on! You've got the key, Kate?"

"Yes, Josh, I do." I held up the ring of keys. "Now to find the right one. I suppose it should be a big one."

It turned out, it was. The door hadn't been opened for years — decades? — and it took some persuasion to get it to move, but I didn't want to force it and damage the woodwork. Or maybe I was enjoying annoying Josh by taking my time. Finally the door yielded with some ominous creaks and squeaks, and we stepped into the dim and dusty space.

As I had expected, there wasn't a lot to see. The ceiling was twenty feet or so above our heads, and a few of the boards above had rotted and splintered. The floor in front of us was poured concrete that hadn't weathered well. The big windows were draped with cobwebs, but they still allowed ample light for our needs. A couple of the windows had broken panes, and dry leaves had blown in here and there. I spotted one dead bird lying on the floor, but it looked like it had been there for a long time. And in the center of the floor there was . . . not much. Some large rusty bolts protruded from where they were embedded in the concrete, marking the outlines of long-lost machinery. I had no idea what kind of machines were required to make shovels.

I glanced at Josh to see how he was reacting to the scene. He was scanning the interior with an intense gaze — but what was he looking for?

"Josh?" I said.

He shook himself as though coming out of a trance. "We never saw anything like an office or a workspace at the mansion, right?"

"Not any place someone could work, even in the basement. I think the library in the house was more for show than for function. Carroll and I checked out the basement again, but there wasn't much to see. Why?"

"So if Henry was working on something, it wasn't at the house or the carriage house. Ergo, it has to be here, unless he had some hidden office in the woods somewhere."

If Henry's secret interest existed at all —

but why rain on Josh's parade? "Okay," I said cautiously. "Assume Henry was working on something. Was he keeping it secret, do you think?"

"Maybe. Look, I know I'm stringing together a lot of assumptions, some wilder than others, and if we don't find anything we can lay it to rest. But I want to know. What's upstairs?"

"Josh, as I keep telling you, I don't know. I don't know how anybody makes shovels. I don't know how much room it takes. I don't know where you put them while waiting to ship them out, or how you ship them. I certainly don't know what the production line would have looked like. I simply don't know any of this."

"You think I do?" he protested. "Actually, I'm looking for a space that was probably smaller than the production floor, but that allowed our Henry room to spread out and work. Where could he have fit in something like that?"

I glanced at Carroll, who was now looking critically at the corners of the room. "I assume there's no basement here?"

"I doubt it," Josh said. "And an attic might be too hot to work in for any length of time in the summer, and too cold in the winter. Which leaves us with the next floor up." He took off for a set of stairs at the side of the building at a near run, without consulting us.

Carroll and I followed more slowly.

"You think he's gone nuts?" Carroll whispered.

"I really don't know," I told her in the same tone. "Maybe he's got writer's block and he's trying to jump-start his brain. But we're here, so we might as well follow him. This shouldn't take long." We trudged up the staircase. Josh was standing at the top, sweeping his gaze over the interior space on the second floor. Across the far end there was a substantial wooden partition, interrupted by some windows and doors, which stretched the entire width of the building. He hurried across the floor, heedless of any weak or broken boards, until he was standing in front of the central door of the partition.

He turned toward me and asked, "You have a key for this?"

"You know I have keys, but I don't know if I have *this* key. But we can find out."

Once again I pulled out the bulky ring of keys and starting sorting through them. The door was only slightly larger than an interior house door, which narrowed down my key hunt to only three or four possibilities. I started trying them, and when I reached the third key it turned in the lock. Did I want to find out what was on the other side of the door?

"You open it, Josh." I stepped away from the door.

He looked at me quizzically, then moved past me and tried to push the door open. It didn't move. He pushed again, harder, and it shifted maybe half an inch.

"Don't break it, Josh," I said. "This may be part of the town's history."

"You think I don't know that?" He leaned carefully against the door until it moved another half inch, and then it sprang open suddenly and he nearly fell into the darkness beyond. There were no windows on the back side of the room, which was the exterior brick wall, so the only light came from the work floor. I reached into my bag and pulled out my cell phone, then found the flashlight app and turned it on. I was almost afraid to look — it would be so disappointing if this space turned out to be the trash room, or where old shovels went to die. But I needed to know, so I turned the phone toward the room.

My first impression was of glints of light. That didn't make any sense. I took a cautious step into the room and something crunched under my feet. I pivoted the phone so the light fell on the floor. Glass. Small shards of glass. Too thin to have been from a broken window, and all the windows appeared to be intact. I carefully picked up one shard: it was slightly curved. Taken all together, it was like a lot of wineglasses had been smashed in a fit of anger. Or maybe there had been a factory closing party, with the same result.

And then my brain made a leap: lightbulbs.

When I looked at Josh, standing next to me, he was grinning like a fool. "I was right!" he crowed.

"About what?" I demanded, still in the dark, in a manner of speaking.

"Henry Barton was experimenting with electric lighting."

"Oh," I said, vaguely disappointed. "I thought Thomas Edison took care of that, and General Electric."

"No, no, no! The scene was much more complicated than that in the 1880s and 1890s. There were a lot of start-ups competing to be first, best, cheapest, you name it. It's one of the more fascinating periods of local, national, and international industry in the nineteenth century. The competition was fierce. Companies merged and split and sold out to one another. Some gave up, some diversified, and some went on to become, as you mentioned, General Electric, which came about through the merger of several companies over time. Yes, Edison was part of that, but you'll notice his name didn't end up on the company because it wasn't his alone. But he got a lot of the credit, and he was incredibly prolific."

"Slow down, Josh! Did you have reason to think that our Henry was involved in all this?"

He was still grinning. "One clue. One small reference in an obscure article that maybe only twelve people in the world have read — that's what pointed me in this direction. And it all comes back to the money. Look, Edison was a brilliant inventor and a great promoter, but a lousy businessman. He kept expanding faster than he could finance, so he ended up selling some of the smaller companies, and more important, some of the patents, to raise more funds for his never-ending research."

I finally made the connection. "And you think Henry owned at least one of those patents? An important one?"

"That or he made significant improvements to it under his own name."

"Why doesn't anybody know about this?"

"Henry worked alone. He wasn't ambitious or particularly competitive. He wasn't living in the hub of all the industrial activity in the area. Still, he appears to have had a good mind, so he started tinkering. I'll bet if we poke around in this building, we'll find some early wiring, and maybe even some intact light bulb prototypes."

"Assuming all that's true, why did he stop? He could have taken on Edison, or even collaborated with him."

"So far the only answer I've come up with is that he lost interest when Mary died — we've already guessed it could be a serious depression. So whatever he made or improved upon after that never went to market, he had no desire to fight with Edison, and he had no sons to leave that part of the business to. I don't know for sure, but I think we can find out."

Finally Carroll spoke. "You're saying that we're looking for Henry Barton's patents?"

"That's right."

"Do you know if they even exist?" Carroll pressed.

"No, but I haven't had a chance to look. I only came upon this reference I mentioned recently. What I need to do is either get online with the patent office, or go to D.C. and take a look for myself. I'm pretty sure

Edison didn't talk about his financial state. Or maybe he thought one or another patent wasn't worth anything and didn't mind unloading it at the time. As I said, there was a lot of competition back in those days, and a lot of what looked like great ideas didn't pan out and were forgotten."

"Why does this matter to you?" Carroll asked. "I mean, you've been saying all along that academically you're more interested in the big picture — the history of regional development, not limited to electrification, although I'll concede that the availability of power made a lot of things possible, so there must have been a lot of business opportunities. But as you said, Henry wasn't exactly mainstream, and he didn't seem to want to promote whatever he might have found. Or maybe none of his ideas worked anyway and he just dropped the whole idea."

Josh looked frustrated. "You could be right, Carroll, but I still want to see if there was any documentation. I know whatever I find might end up as an obscure footnote in somebody else's book, but I need to know. Look, we still haven't found any documents in this building, but we aren't done looking. Let's do a thorough search and be done with it. If we don't find anything, I can't think of anywhere else to look, so we'll just close the book on it. Is that okay with you two?"

Carroll and I glanced at each other, and I spoke first. "We can give it until dark, I guess — we didn't think to bring any flashlights or anything."

"It may not even take that long," Josh insisted. "Look around — there aren't a lot of places where you could put a stash of paper records. Certainly not downstairs on the ground floor. We can check out this space, and then look for any office-type rooms. Surely there must have been a few managers here when it was a shovel factory, right? And after?"

I didn't feel like arguing with him. Besides, he was right. It wouldn't take long. "Sure, fine. Let's do it."

"Then let's split up. We might have missed something downstairs. Carroll, you want to take that? Kate and I can split up the space up here."

"Fine," Carroll said, sounding a bit testy. I couldn't blame her. It had been a long day for both of us. I found myself almost hoping that we *didn't* find anything, so we could just go home and take a nap.

Carroll dutifully went down the stairs. Josh pointed at one end of the long, narrow room we were standing in and said, "You take that end, and I'll take this one. Start at the outside wall and work inward, and we'll meet in the middle." He marched off without saying anything else, so I just followed his instructions.

There were shelves along the outside wall, and on the shelves there were wooden boxes, so I made a guess that nobody had used this room since the invention and widespread use of cardboard boxes, whenever the heck that was. I knew nothing about what circumstances had closed the factory down. That had been long after Henry's death in 1911, and before I was born. Who had taken over the place? Had it remained a factory or had it been used only for storage? Someone had cleared out the machinery, whatever it had been. Presumably all of this information was recorded somewhere in town, either at the library or in the town offices somewhere. As far as I knew, the town hadn't sold the factory building, although they might have been able to rent it out and make a little money from it. It was likely that both the power and the water had long since been shut off, so maintenance of the building couldn't have cost much. How sad that no one had wanted the place, and no one had even wanted the underlying land enough to raze the building and put in something more functional.

I reached the end of the room and contemplated my options. There were a few wooden boxes, but they didn't appear to be nailed shut. Nor were they labeled. And — I had to blink a few times to make sure I was seeing what I thought — there was a large antique safe tucked in the corner, its front flush with the brick wall, almost obscured by the boxes. I hauled a couple of the boxes out of the way and tried the handle. Naturally it was locked. But the massive thing did not have a combination lock, only a keyhole. And I had large ring of keys. What were the odds that one of them fit? Why not find out?

I sat down cross-legged on the floor in front of the large hunk of metal. I debated about saying a short prayer, but I couldn't think of an appropriate one, so I just started trying the keys. When one finally fit in the keyhole I was startled, and more so when it turned and something inside the safe clicked. I paused for a moment, wondering how I'd feel if it turned out to be empty. Then I said to myself, "Chicken," grabbed the handle, and pulled. Then I stared at the stacks of yellowed paper that nearly filled the interior.

Finally I stood up carefully and called out, "Josh? I think I've got something."

# 20

Josh arrived quickly, then skidded to a stop. "Holy crap!" he said in a reverent voice.

I almost laughed at his rare use of profanity. "Crap, maybe, but I doubt it's holy. I didn't touch anything, so you can do the honors."

He knelt in front of the open safe, and I scooched over to give him space. Josh reached into the safe and pulled out a clutch of papers, handling them reverently. He began leafing through them, so I stood up, went out to the stairwell, and called out for Carroll. She answered quickly. "What?" she demanded, walking into the main space of the ground floor room below.

"I think we've struck the mother lode. You'd better come and check things out, before Josh has a heart attack."

"Thank goodness! All I've found are some very large spiders."

I turned back to the long room where Josh

hadn't moved an inch, and Carroll followed shortly. She and I both sat on the floor, watching Josh. We must have looked like primitive worshippers. Of bits of paper?

"Well?" Carroll said impatiently, after several minutes of silence.

Josh looked up at her as if surprised to see her there. "Business records, and not for the shovel works. If there is any justice in the world, there will be copies of the patents in this pile somewhere."

"Congratulations, I guess," I said. "What does that mean?"

"It means that I might be able to contribute a small piece of history — assuming that all this is what I think it is. I'm glad you're here, Carroll — you can help me look through this stuff. If you need to get up to speed on the nineteenth-century state of electrification, I've got some books I can lend you."

My brain was working sluggishly. "I don't mean to be crass, but are these worth anything financially — setting aside their historic importance?"

"As old documents? Maybe, but not a lot. Carroll would know more about that side than I do. But . . ."

It was kind of fun watching different expressions drift across Josh's face as he worked out the implications of a possible major find. "I'm no expert on the legal issues," he began carefully, "but it is possible that if some of these patents predate Edison's claims, or if Edison had sold them to Henry, they could have some value that might go beyond the financial. There could be broader implications."

Was he being deliberately vague? "It's worth checking, isn't it?" I prompted.

"I think so. I'd guess if Henry had some sort of prior claim, it would be one heck of a lawsuit that would probably last longer than any of us. It might depend on who inherited Henry's assets. Kate, you've said that the town owns it all, at least until it was sold, which never happened. That would be a real long shot."

"We'd need a lawyer to sort that out, I'm guessing," I said. "But there's another aspect: think of the negative PR the current electric moguls, or whoever used the Edison patents, would get for fighting with a dead man."

Josh thought for a moment, then said slowly, "Well, let's climb out on a limb and say it's Mid-Atlantic Power that benefited. And now a hundred-plus years later they find they don't own the rights to the patents that launched their company."

"An honest mistake?" I asked. "As far as I know, MAP's been doing business for a long time, and they have a good record. And don't forget, the patent trail might be difficult to follow. And things get lost. Or maybe Henry never bothered to file the patents in his name, if all he wanted was something to tinker with. Or maybe MAP stiffed Henry Barton?" I added. "It's possible, isn't it?"

"I suppose," he said. "There are a lot of possibilities."

Carroll spoke up suddenly. "You two — you're forgetting one thing here."

Josh and I turned to her in unison. "What?"

"Zach Mitchell. He's dead, remember?"

"What does that have to do with any of this?" I asked.

"Think about it. Kate, you told me this has always been a peaceful town. Then this Zach shows up in town here for no apparent reason, less than a week ago. He doesn't know anyone around here, and they don't seem to know him. There sure isn't much to do in this town, so he's unlikely to be a tourist. He comes snooping around the library, and he claims to be looking for family history information. Okay, that's credible — genealogists can be kind of obsessive."

When I started to protest, she kept going. "But! Then he apparently breaks into the library, and he ends up dead. Doesn't that seem just a bit too coincidental?"

"Carroll, are you're suggesting that he was looking for information on Henry Barton? And the only thing of value associated with Henry might — just maybe — be the patents that we're looking for? Is that what you're asking?"

"That's my theory," Carroll said.

"That seems kind of far-fetched," Josh observed. "All this is pretty obscure stuff."

"Yes, but the man is dead, and even the state police believe that it wasn't an accident. There has to be a good reason."

"Somebody thought he was worth killing," I added.

Josh was beginning to sound testy when he said, "But why? He was a graduate student. He'd never been here before."

"Then maybe we're missing something," I told him. "*Somebody* killed him."

"Then ask your detective pal — he should have found something more on the victim."

"I hope so," I replied. "But Detective Reynolds has no reason to connect the dots between Zach and Henry Barton's files. Maybe we do."

"Okay, say this Zach did make some sort

of connection. What would he do with that information? Who would he talk to?" Josh said.

I thought it was a reasonable question, but I didn't have an answer. Josh kept talking.

"I think you're getting ahead of yourself here," he went on. "Talk to Reynolds, ask him if he knows anything more about Zach now, or if he's held something back. In the meantime, we need to decide what to do with this new find just in case it turns out to be as important as we think it may be."

I wasn't sure my tired brain was up to sorting out what was where, and who knew where we'd put it. "I'm going to assume that leaving it here isn't an option. This place has no security. What's the best option?"

"Guys?" Carroll spoke up. "Maybe there's someone else involved in this search. Could be an accomplice, could be a competitor."

"Good thought, Carroll," I told her. Although I had trouble believing that two people had come up with the same idea about the Barton patents as we did, at the same time. Maybe an accomplice who got greedy and didn't want to split the profits, if there were any? "But who do we look for?"

The three of us sat on the floor and

silently tried to sort through what facts we had. After a while Carroll asked, "It's still Sunday, isn't it?"

"I think so," I said. "Why?"

"Well, neither the town hall nor the bank will be open, so we can't stash this stuff at either one of those. We already believe that the library is not a safe place. Any other ideas?"

"Hand it over to Ryan?" I said. "He's a lawyer. So far I haven't told him anything about all this, but he works for a law firm, where I assume they keep plenty of legal documents."

"What would you tell him?"

"In theory I don't have to tell him anything — just that we've found some documents in the Barton papers that we think might be valuable or important or something like that and we want to keep them safe."

"Would he accept that excuse?"

"Probably. Look, I'd like to take them over to the state police HQ, but I think explaining why we were there would take half the night and leave them laughing," I said glumly.

Finally Josh got frustrated. He stood up abruptly and said, "Okay, I vote that we take these boxes to the B&B, and we all stay there tonight keeping an eye on them. Then in the morning you can ask Ryan to take them someplace safe. And one more person will know they exist."

I didn't have the energy to argue. "Fine. We're all punch-drunk and I can't think of anything better. But don't you dare stop and read any of them. I want to get out of here before dark."

# 21

"Amen," Carroll said. "But there's one small problem: we walked here. We need a vehicle, and all of ours are parked near the library."

"I'll go get mine," Josh volunteered. "I'm sure there's room in the trunk for the contents of the safe."

"Fine, let the womenfolk do all the heavy work," I said. When Josh looked confused I told him, "Just go and get your car. We'll get the documents out of the safe and into boxes so they won't be damaged. But you can carry the boxes down the stairs."

"Right," he said. Newly energized, he loped down the stairs, and I heard the outer door open and close.

I turned back to Carroll. "If I weren't so exhausted, I guess I'd be excited. But we still have to stash these somewhere at the B&B. Let's get things packed up so we're ready to go. Since you're the expert, I'll clean out some boxes and you can fill them. Let's get started."

After all that we'd already shuffled around over the past couple of days, this batch was surprisingly easy to manage, and we had everything swapped out quickly. Josh returned and started transferring the boxes to the trunk of his car. I told him to keep an eye on the street in all directions, to make sure no one was paying attention to us. Okay, maybe that was paranoid, and there were three of us, but I preferred to be safe than sorry, so I could find out if we were on the right track about Henry.

When everything was stowed in the car, Josh said, "Now what?"

"Carroll and I have to get our cars at the library. You drop us there, and take the boxes to the B&B. We'll be right behind you. Then I'll call Ryan to see if he's willing to take them to his office. If not, we sit on them — all of us — until the bank opens in the morning."

"I agree," Josh said. "I'll drop you at your cars and go on to the B&B and wait for you there."

The streets were as empty as they had been earlier in the day, and I didn't spot anyone giving us the evil eye as we passed. On our way to the library, a thought hit me.

"Damn, I forgot about Eric. What do we do if he's at the B&B? Or he's still with Ryan?"

Josh spoke up. "Let's hope he's somewhere else. If his car's at the B&B I'll wait in my car until you two arrive, and you can reconnoiter. If he's not around, we should get the boxes out of sight before he shows up."

I was too tired to argue. "Fine, that's what we'll do." And we did: no car, no Eric, and we scurried into the B&B like busy ants clutching the boxes and stashed them in the pantry off the kitchen. Then we collapsed in the parlor.

"A brilliant plan," Josh said, his head lolling against the chair cushions behind him, his eyes closed.

"Thank you." I could feel my own eyelids drooping.

"We're tired and hungry and I'd really like a shower," Carroll said. "If anyone breaks in looking for our stash of precious documents, I won't have the energy to fight with them. For now they're out of sight. Let's get some food into us so we can think straight."

"And then we'll fall asleep and the elves will come and spirit away the historical find of the century," Josh said with a sneer. I glared at him and he raised his hand.

"Sorry, I'm getting loopy. You're right — we aren't cut out for this."

"What time is it?" I asked after a long yawn.

"After seven," Carroll said. "It'll be dark in, what, an hour?"

"Maybe," I told her. "By nine, anyway."

"Kate, you know your way around the town," Carroll said. "You go get food."

"Fine. Requests?"

"Go to the supermarket and get whatever looks good and is quick."

"Yes, ma'am!" I hauled myself out of my nice comfy chair, turned on my heel, headed for the door, retrieved my car, and pointed myself toward the supermarket on the fringe of town, more or less on autopilot. It would take a little more time than looking for a place to find real food in town, but I was pretty sure that on a Sunday evening there wouldn't be much open.

The market was still open, if not for long, and there were few people in it. I grabbed up the components for our go-to meal — pasta, jarred sauce, and grated cheese — and tossed them into my basket. Then I remembered we had nothing for breakfast, and the supply of coffee was getting pretty low, so I went back and grabbed some more stuff. When I finally made it to the checkout,

I noticed that the sky was overcast and it was getting dark fast. Time to go.

With next to no traffic in town, I made it back to the B&B quickly. There was definitely a storm coming. The first raindrops hit the windshield as I pulled into the parking area behind the building. I gathered up my bags and scurried into the house.

"Food!" I announced brightly. "Who's cooking?"

"I guess I should," Carroll said. "You've done it more often than I have."

"Thank you. I need to call Ryan about stashing the stuff. Any sign of Eric?"

"Nope. I'm beginning to think he's a ghost."

"Well, at least he doesn't expect to be entertained. Or even fed. Let me know if you need anything, and I'll go make my phone call."

I tried Ryan first. He didn't answer his cell, and I figured it was too late for him to be in his office, and I had no idea what his home number was, so I settled for leaving a message on his cell. "Ryan, it's Kate. I need to talk to you about the Barton papers, ideally early tomorrow. Please call me."

One thing checked off my list. Now what? Sunday evening was not an ideal time to try to reach people, not that I blamed them for ducking my calls. I made a mental note to call Detective Reynolds in the morning, since I had new information to share with him. Then I sat behind Cordy's former desk and stared into space for a while. I was pretty sure that the papers we'd found at the factory were potentially important, but I had no idea what to do next. At the same time, I was reluctant to share information with too many more people, because it seemed all too probable that somebody had killed Zach for those papers. What should I do?

That was as far as I'd gotten when I heard a key in the lock, and then Eric walked in. I felt a moment of panic: I didn't want Carroll and Josh blabbing about our adventures that day, so I'd have to intercept Eric and remind Carroll and Josh to keep their mouths shut.

"Eric!" I greeted him when I reached the hallway. "You are the perfect guest, because I never see you and you never ask for anything. Are you going out with Ryan tonight? Or would you rather join us for dinner? Nothing fancy, but there should be plenty."

"That's very kind of you. I hadn't realized that this was one of those towns that rolled up the sidewalks at night. Let me go drop my things in my room upstairs. Give me five."

"Fine." I waited until he was out of earshot, then dashed to the kitchen. "The mysterious Eric just showed up, and I invited him to eat with us. Just don't say anything about the factory or the Barton collections, please!"

Eric appeared a few minutes later. At the kitchen door he greeted Carroll and Josh. "Something smells good," he said.

"Hasn't Ryan been feeding you?" I asked.

"Yes, but he does have work to do. I've been following a few military campaigns around the countryside, stopping when I feel like it. It's a pleasant change from the corporate life."

"Did much happen around here during the Civil War? I apologize for my ignorance, but I've never been very interested in local history," I told him.

"Actually, yes. Some of the Confederate forces retreated through here after the Battle of Gettysburg in 1863. The Northern soldiers were almost out of ammunition when reinforcements arrived. So there were a few active days."

"I did not know that. Is there a military cemetery nearby?"

"That I couldn't say — I haven't had

enough time around here. Aren't you from around here?"

"I was, but I left after high school, and I was never into cemeteries, I've worked in other places since then — Baltimore most recently, and Philadelphia before that."

Eric smiled. "Really? I'm originally from the Philadelphia area, or right outside the city."

"Carroll mentioned that."

"I'm working on a graduate degree at Penn," Carroll told him, and she stirred something vigorously. "I'm just visiting Kate here — we met not long ago. Will you be around in the morning? Maybe we can chat then."

"I'd enjoy that, but Ryan said something about plans. Let's wait and see, shall we?"

"Sure." Carroll turned to me. "Food's almost ready."

"Can we eat in the kitchen?" Josh asked plaintively. "It seems like too much work to set the table in the dining room."

"I won't object," Eric said, laughing.

I retrieved another bottle of Cordy's wine — I'd be sorry when they were all gone — and brought it back to the kitchen, while Josh and Carroll dished up.

When we were settled, I said, "Eric, what do you do when you're not chasing soldiers around the countryside?"

"I'm a vice president in management at a major electric company in Delaware. Far more interesting than the dairy business."

Somewhere inside my head, a little alarm bell was ringing. "Would that be Mid-Atlantic?"

"Yes. We provide service for this area."

"I thought it sounded familiar, but as I said, it's been a long time since I lived around here, and things change. And I wasn't paying the electric bills when I was in high school."

"The company has been in business for close to a century. Actually, it came about from the merger of a number of smaller regional companies, and we've added a few since then. We're one of the largest in the country now. I've been with them for going on twenty years now, and I came up through the ranks."

"How interesting," Carroll said. "I've learned a bit about Philadelphia's water department, since I've been spending time there getting a degree. Do you know, there are still bits and pieces of the original city piping? They were made up of logs — or more like tree trunks — lined with lead. Hard to imagine supplying a city like that."

"There's a lot of history to Philadelphia,"

Eric said. "Have you seen Bartram's Garden, south of the city, near the airport? That was one of the earlier commercial sources for plants in the region."

I was relieved that Carroll had diverted the conversation. I was still chewing over the fact that Eric worked for Mid-Atlantic, but my brain was too mushy to ask him any questions about it without making a mess of it. I planned to talk with Ryan in the morning, so maybe I could pump him for information about his old friend. And if it seemed relevant, I could tell Detective Reynolds. Eric seemed like a very nice guy, but he'd been kind of secretive since he'd arrived in the Asheboro area.

Carroll nudged me. "Kate, you ready to go up?"

I looked at my watch and was shocked to see that it was nearly eleven. "I'm surprised my eyes are still open. We've had a busy day. Let me lock up. Eric, you're welcome to stay down here and read or something."

"Thanks, Kate, but I'm about ready to turn in myself. See you in the morning." Eric headed for the stairs, while I went around the first floor checking that doors were locked and lights were turned off and that the alarm system was active.

Carroll was following hard on my heels.

"He wasn't giving much away, was he?" she said in a low voice. "Interesting that he's part of the local electric company, isn't it? And he hadn't mentioned it before."

"It is, though I don't know what it means yet. Just as well. I left a message for Ryan, and I'll leave one for the detective now, and I hope they'll call early. I think the police should know we found the Barton papers and that they're safe, and also about who Eric is. Maybe it means nothing, but I'd like to know that someone else knows, if you know what I mean."

"I know you need some sleep," Carroll said, smiling. "Maybe you'll be making more sense in the morning."

"I hope so. I left a message for Ryan and asked him to call me in the morning. I need to see if he can stash the documents somewhere safe."

"You mean you won't let me and Josh dig into our new documents?" Carroll summoned up a smile.

"Not yet! I hope we'll get things sorted out in the next couple of days, and then you two can go to town. Just don't talk about them to anyone else, okay?"

Carroll sighed theatrically. "If you insist."

"For now I do. Have patience!" I told her.

"Good night, then." She headed for the stairs.

Josh had somehow disappeared while Carroll and I had been talking, and I found him slumped in an upholstered chair in the parlor. He was asleep. Eric had gone upstairs, so I shook Josh's shoulder.

He jerked to a half-awake state. "Wha?"

"Bedtime. You're staying, right?"

"If you want."

"I do. We're guarding the papers, remember? Carroll and Eric have already gone up."

He lurched to his feet and all but fell against me. Deliberately? I didn't know — or care. I was glad he was here, and glad we'd made at least some small progress with the Barton documents — and with finding out why Zach Mitchell had died. I hoped that Detective Reynolds could fill in some of the gaps in the morning.

"Upstairs, Josh. Tomorrow will be another busy day."

We both headed up the stairs and crashed.

# 22

I pried my eyes open far too early the next morning — blast that early June sun! It seemed to be Monday, the day many people counted as the first day of the week. What the heck had been on my calendar for this week? The town meeting had been a week ago. Carroll had arrived Thursday morning, and then we found the body at the library. Since then, Josh, Carroll, and I had been running around all over town, sorting documents, moving documents, looking for still more documents, which we had found but still didn't quite know what to do with. Now it was Monday, and the state police still didn't know who had killed Zach Mitchell or why, and we had another pile of documents to go through and no more space to hold them. I'd told Carroll that Ryan would be calling me back — I hoped! — and if he couldn't help, I would stop in at the bank and see if they had some sort of mega-vault that would hold all the boxes for now. After all this effort, and one dead body, I wanted to be sure they were safe.

I decided that I was fully awake and might as well get out of bed. And make coffee. Coffee was the one constant in my rapidly changing world. I stumbled down the stairs to find that Carroll had beaten me to it. "I see you found the coffee. What about the muffins?"

"In the oven warming," Carroll said.

No sign of Josh or Eric. That was fine with me. "You think it's too early to talk to Ryan?"

"No idea," Carroll said. "How do you want us to handle the factory documents?"

"I assume by 'us' you mean you and Josh, not me. Let's wait and see if Ryan has any room for them. I don't think we should leave them in the house without somebody here. Will you and Josh be okay working on your own?"

"Well, that leaves you today to line up a safe place for the papers."

"I'm less worried about the Barton papers than I am about having an unknown killer on the prowl in Asheboro. We might be a little closer to figuring out who killed Zach, but I don't think anybody has enough evidence to arrest anybody. Ideally I'd like to get all this wrapped up soon so I can get back to what I'm supposed to be doing. I'm being a good cheerleader for the project, but considering we have no plan and no money to implement it and I still haven't talked to most of the people in town about it, I'm not optimistic about the chances for success. I'll be the first to concede that I'm not a miracle worker."

"Don't forget you keep finding bodies — that can't help," Carroll said. "Are you having fun?"

"Apart from the bodies part, yes. I love the idea of reviving the old town, and I think it's possible, but it's going to mean a lot of work from a lot of people."

"And you win them all over to your vision of the place," Carroll said, smiling.

"Well, I hope so."

Josh was next to appear. He was looking a little worn, even though he should have been psyched to dig into the newly discovered Barton documents. "Coffee?" Josh asked plaintively. I pointed to the pot on the table.

"Any signs of life from Eric?" I asked him.

"Nope. But his car's gone," Josh told me.

I hadn't noticed. He certainly was an elusive person. "Wow, he really is serious about this Civil War stuff. My idea of a vacation is *not* getting up at dawn. So, Carroll has already given me orders for the day. You and she are going to tackle the papers we found at the factory, while I go and sweet-talk the bank or some equivalent like Ryan to provide us with a safe place to store them. At no time should the papers be left unprotected. Do you agree?"

Josh had swallowed half his cup of coffee. "You sure you aren't overreacting?"

"I'd rather overreact than lose the whole lot of them. And it's not for long. You two should be able to get through them quickly, right?"

Josh nodded. "We should be able to make a first pass at them today, and figure out what we need to know about patent law. Think Ryan could help?"

"Maybe. He's on my to-call list for this morning, if he doesn't call me first. I left him a message yesterday, and Detective Reynolds too."

"You haven't heard anything new from him?" Josh asked.

"No." I'd been so exhausted the night before that I hadn't had time to really think about what Detective Reynolds had told me. It sounded as though he had found out most of the easily available information about Zach, but little more. I wasn't sure he grasped the full significance of the Barton papers, if they were in fact connected to Zach's death, but why should he? It was a pretty narrow area of specialization, and apparently Henry Barton's importance a century ago had not extended as far as state police headquarters. He was probably wondering what all the fuss was about. But even I knew that people could kill for the most trivial and absurd of reasons.

"Earth to Kate?" I heard Carroll saying as if from a great distance.

"Huh? What?"

"We're about ready to get started. What time does the bank open?"

"I, uh, don't remember. Probably by nine, anyway."

"You have someone you know there, who you can speak to?"

"Not exactly." Since the former bank president had been summarily fired for embezzlement and was now awaiting trial. "But it's not a big place, and even if I don't know the staff, they should know who I am. So, how much space will we need?"

"Bigger than a safe-deposit box. Maybe the size of a standard footlocker? For just the factory documents."

"Okay, that people should recognize. Anybody need more food? Coffee?" I stood up. "Why don't I grab the first shower, since I have to go to the bank and look like a respectable grown-up."

"Kate, just go get ready," Josh said. "If we need anything else we can call you on your cell."

He was being annoying, but he had a point: I had things to do, and they needed time and space to do what they were doing. "Let me know when you finish with the papers and we can discuss moving them."

Half an hour later I was standing in the bank trying to explain to a manager only a few years older than I was what I was looking for. "I have several large wooden boxes of financial documents that may be valuable, and I want to put them in a safe place for a short time."

"How large is large?" the manager asked.

"Three cubic boxes, each about two feet square. They probably weight twenty pounds apiece. It's just papers, no objects. I'm guessing about a footlocker's worth."

"Our safe deposit boxes are nowhere near that big. Have you considered a commercial storage facility?"

I gritted my teeth. "As I said, these are potentially important documents. They are also over a century old and therefore fragile. I need to store them for a short period of time. All I'm asking is whether you can provide a secure place to keep them until I can find a final home for them."

"What about a lawyer's office?" the manager volunteered.

"Where do most lawyers you know keep their legal documents like wills and such?"

"Uh, here, at the bank. They probably keep a copy at their office as well."

This was getting ridiculous. I could have left them in the safe at the factory and saved myself the trouble. I pasted on a smile. "Thank you for the information. I think I might call a lawyer, since you don't seem to offer any appropriate options." I turned on my heel and walked out before I said something I'd regret. And then I called Ryan from the sidewalk.

"Hey, Kate," he answered in a cheerful voice. "What's up? Anything new?"

"Ryan, did you get my message? I'm looking for a place to stash some of the Barton papers that may be valuable, and the bank doesn't seem to have any appropriate space."

"You can't keep them at the B&B?"

"That doesn't seem to be a good option, in terms of security. Where does your law firm keep important documents?"

"On-site, mostly, in a modern safe. How

big are you talking?"

"Carroll said about the size of a footlocker."

"Oh. I was picturing maybe one bankers' box."

"Henry Barton kept a *lot* of records. Can you help?"

"Let me nose around and see what space we have. Why don't we meet for lunch and catch up?"

"Fine. At the hotel?"

"Great. Noon all right with you?"

"Perfect. See you there."

So now it was ten o'clock and I had two hours to kill. There was nothing useful I could do back at the B&B and I'd probably be in the way, so I decided to use the time to explore the center of town some more, and maybe talk to a few of the shopkeepers I hadn't met yet. I really needed to bring a decent camera with me, so I could record the shops in their current condition, which would give me an idea of what would need to be changed and what could get by with no more than a cleanup and a coat of paint.

I sat down on a bench in the heart of town and surveyed what I seemed to have proclaimed to be my domain. It was a pleasant view, if you could ignore the peeling paint and broken shingles and shabby signage.

But those were superficial and could be fixed. What would draw people into the town? Food, of course — but 1900 food or twenty-first-century food? I doubted parents would bring young children to a place like I envisioned, so maybe I could go for a more upscale adult menu, with a few historic dishes. Gift shops? I'd been to more than my share of museums and other attractions, both in the States and abroad, and I had fairly strong ideas about what I would like to see. But I'd brought home plenty of souvenirs, and if the vendors chose well they could be tasteful, not throwaway junk. Maybe there were local artists who would like to maintain a small sales gallery somewhere, possibly in combination with a different kind of shop.

And what was the 1900 equivalent of a porta-potty, or whatever they called it back then? People needed someplace to go, whatever the era, but where to put them? And where did visitors, local or from a distance, "park" their horse and carriage?

I was startled when Mayor Skip dropped down on the bench next to me. "Hey, Kate. Did you get everything moved?"

I decided not to mention the documents from the factory. "We did, and thank you for finding the people to help, starting with

Beverly, who did a great job getting a crew together. We'll have to put together a small exhibit so people can see what they were lugging around." I reminded myself to check if Henry had kept any photographs. Or maybe the library collections included some views of the main street. People liked to look at pictures, right? And it made sense to show them what life was like back then, than to hand them a brochure and tell them to go away and read it. There were always details that people didn't even think of.

"Aren't you supposed to be at the school, Skip?"

"Dentist appointment." He pointed toward his chin. "Chipped a molar over the weekend, but I'm allowing myself a few minutes to play hooky. Let's hope no students see me. How's the planning going?"

"In fits and starts. My friend is going through the documents to see what else Henry Barton kept. The attic at the mansion is now cleared out so we can see what needs to be done up there, if anything. Of course, this latest death has complicated things."

"You really can't catch a break, can you?" Skip appeared sympathetic.

"Bad karma? How many murders has this town had, as long as you've been here?"

"Since I was a kid? Uh, three, maybe — until you arrived. And one of those was a guy who was shot somewhere else and managed to drive into town before expiring. Does that count? You know, you should talk to Frances Carter at the newspaper. All their archives are still there, and I'm sure Frances would be happy to work with you."

"That's a great idea, Skip." Why hadn't I thought of that? I wondered if they had any pictures of the factory when it was operating. Or any pictures of Henry and his wife.

Skip stood up. "I guess duty calls. Let me know if you need anything else."

"Thanks, Skip; I really appreciate your help. I want to involve as many people from town as I can, which will make everyone's work load easier."

"You got it! Bye now." He strode off toward a parked car. I still had an hour to kill before I was supposed to meet Ryan, and the hotel was no more than a ten-minute drive away, although in a different town. *Maybe I should start the ball rolling at the newspaper.* I really should have thought of it sooner, but I'd been kind of distracted.

I crossed the street to the building where the newspaper had been housed as long as I could remember. It was on the second floor, so I climbed the creaky wooden stairs and opened the door, which still bore the gilt lettering that proudly proclaimed *The Asheboro Chronicle.* Inside there was an eight-foot counter facing the door, and a scattering of mismatched desks that all held computer terminals, monitors, and printers. There was only one human, a seventy-ish woman who looked vaguely familiar.

She stepped up to the counter, grinning. "Kate Hamilton. I wondered when you'd get around to visiting me."

# 23

"Sorry — Mrs. Carter, is it? I should have figured you'd know everything about the town."

"Not quite as far back as you're looking for, but we've got plenty of things to look at. We were lucky to get a state grant to digitize our collections a few years back. I think the agency that gave us the money liked us because we were small and came cheap."

"So you still have it all?"

"Sure do. What're you looking for?"

"Right now, anything to do with Henry Barton. His history, his wife, his house, his factory, even his dog, if he had one. I'm still looking for ideas, and he was the biggest man in town, back in the nineteenth century."

"And his file's still the biggest in our archives. What do you want to see first?"

"You sure you don't have anything else

you need to do right now?"

"In case you haven't heard, we're a weekly now, and I'm the only person who works here — I don't even bother to pay myself anymore. I'm past seventy, but I can't just sit at home and fade away, so I come here. Got some high school kids who help out with formatting and uploading and all that stuff that I've never learned. But if I don't do this, nobody will. Call it a labor of love."

I made an immediate mental note to see what I could do to preserve this treasure. I checked my watch. "Frances, I'm meeting someone for lunch, but I'd really like to see what you have here. Why don't I come back this afternoon? That'll give you time to put together what you have in your files, and we can go over them together. Is that all right?"

"Kate, I have more time than I know what to do with. I'll do what you suggested, and I'll be here all afternoon."

"Thank you! Oh, let me give you my mobile number, in case you have any questions or find something amazing." I scribbled the number on a piece of paper from my purse. "See you later."

Much as I would have loved to have stayed and dug through the archives, I needed to talk to Ryan and make sure he could keep Henry's legal documents safe. I rushed down the stairs and back to my car.

When I hurried into the hotel lobby, I nearly collided with Ryan. We air-kissed perfunctorily and then let ourselves be guided to a table. Ryan ordered a drink, but I asked for iced tea.

"So, how's it going?" Ryan said heartily.

"Apart from an unsolved murder? Great. I've got a lot of ideas."

"B&B still working out for you?"

"For the moment. I have to say I haven't seen much of Eric — he's sort of a ghost."

"What's so mysterious about Eric?"

"Have you seen much of him?"

"Can't say that I have, but that's not unexpected. I've been busy at work, and he's on vacation. What's the problem?"

"Well, he's out of the house before anyone else gets up, and he comes back late. It's not a problem, but he's not the most sociable guy."

"You do understand that 'vacation' means he wants peace and quiet, and he wants to see the battlefields in some sort of order."

"You know him well?" I asked.

"I think I told you earlier that Eric and I went to college together, but then we went our separate ways. Since college we see each other maybe once a year, and swap holiday cards. We're not really close, but we keep in touch. Why the curiosity?"

"I'm just being careful. Let me say that some of the things I've found in the past week are bigger than I'd expected. Did you know he worked for Mid-Atlantic Power?"

"He might have mentioned it. I never gave it much thought. When we get together we don't usually talk business, and he's never asked for legal advice. What does it matter?"

"I don't know that it does, but it may be part of the puzzle. And I may need legal counsel."

"Kate, you're worrying me. Maybe you should start at the beginning."

"Should I hire you as my attorney?"

"If it would make you feel better. Give me a dollar and you'll be my client officially."

I felt a bit silly handing Ryan a crumpled dollar bill, but it did in fact make me feel better. "Okay, let me walk you through it." I started in with the call to Carroll to look at the rest of the Barton papers, and their current but temporary disposition. Then I gave him cursory details about finding the body at the library, and the police response. Somewhere along the way we managed to order lunch, and eat it.

When I reached a stopping point, Ryan

said, "That's all very interesting, but what's it got to do with you and what you're working on? A guy nobody seems to have known was killed in the town library. Unfortunate, but is it relevant to you? The state police are investigating, but they haven't said anything to you about suspects. Although why should they?"

"Because I found the body? Never mind. I didn't know him, nor did Carroll or Josh, so we have nothing to contribute to the police investigation. Actually, there was something else I wanted to talk to you about." I launched into the next phase of the story: the Barton papers from the factory and our off-the-wall theories about who held the rights to the patents. Ryan didn't interrupt. By the time I wrapped up, he was looking a bit stunned. "Well?" I asked.

"Let me get this straight. You — the three of you — believe that Henry Barton in his later years, after he got rich from the shovel business and built his mansion, started dabbling in the world of electricity."

"Yes. At least in lightbulbs."

Ryan nodded once. "And he may have come up with something important, working in the Asheboro factory or he bought a patent or patents from Thomas Edison that turned out to be important. And while this patent, or maybe more than one, might be pivotal to the whole history of the electric industry, it vanished for over a century. It may never have been filed or recorded, or it was lost, or maybe nobody ever looked for them. Nobody remembers anything about it because they're all dead now."

"That about sums it up. It seems possible that there could be quite a bit of money involved. Or maybe not. Josh knows the general history of electrification of the region, but none of us knows much about the legal side of things. But the only reason we can come up with for why Zach Mitchell broke into the library and died is that he was trying to find those same documents."

"That's kind of a leap of logic, Kate. You really think he knew about the patents?"

"Maybe. But he didn't find them before he died because they were stored in a safe in the factory. We found them, and Josh and Carroll are going through the latest batch of papers as we speak."

"So what do you want from me?" Ryan asked.

"Right now, a safe place to store the new documents. We moved them from the factory to the B&B yesterday, but if they are important the B&B is not the best place to keep them, even short term. And the library has no security at all. I asked if the bank could keep them, but they seemed boggled by the idea of storing a trunkful of papers. So I thought of you."

"Have you told the state police about your theory?"

"I plan to do that today. Remember, we only found the documents yesterday afternoon, so the police aren't up to speed on all this yet. And I don't think they'll see the implications of finding a legal document that may have a significant impact on regional power generation and be worth a whole lot of money. They're focusing on the death, as they should. Right now I just want to keep the documents safe until we can figure out what to do. Can you help?"

Ryan smiled. "You know, if you'd just come to me and asked if I could store some papers for you, I could have said yes in a minute. Now I have far too much information."

"But this is merely a hypothesis. I didn't actually give you any firm facts. Do you?"

"Not that I know of. I'm just pointing out that I don't need to know what I'm protecting, certainly not if you're my client, which you are now. Unless of course someone will follow the papers and try to kill me. You would tell me about something like that, wouldn't you?"

"Of course I would. I don't want to see anybody else get hurt or killed. And if all this was just an interesting footnote to history, I wouldn't worry. But if this has important financial impact on certain companies, that raises the stakes, wouldn't you say? And a man is dead."

"Yes. But what are you going to do about it?"

"Josh is a respected scholar of industrial history. Carroll is an expert on the dating and provenance of old documents. I can't think of two better people to handle this. As long as they — and the documents — are safe. If something happens to either of them I'll never forgive myself."

"Where are they now?"

"At the B&B with the documents. They know what the risks are."

Ryan seemed to have arrived at a decision. "All right. Our firm has a walk-in safe — we keep a lot of legal documents on hand, and as you've found out, local banks are not always the best repository. If you can deliver the documents to my office, we will protect them. When will they be available?"

"Josh and Carroll thought they'd have enough of the information they need by this afternoon, so we can hand them over today."

"Do you need help with transport?"

"I'm not sure. Do you have a bonded delivery service or something like that?"

"I can arrange for one. Or I could simply go with you and bring them back myself."

"We could all come with you when you do that. That would be sufficient protection, wouldn't it?"

"You really are worried, Kate, aren't you?" Ryan asked softly.

"To tell the truth, yes. I know I'm in over my head."

"I'll help you take care of it. Even if it means bringing everyone along for the ride," he said, smiling.

"Thank you." I shook myself after my brief flash of sentimental honesty. "Let me call Josh and see how they're doing." When I fished out my cell phone, I saw I had a phone message, but it was a number that I didn't recognize, and I needed to touch base with Josh and Carroll first.

Josh answered quickly. "Checking up on us?" he said, but he sounded cheerful.

"Of course. The bank was a bust, but Ryan has agreed to store the boxes in his office's safe. How close to done are you?"

"Another hour should do it. Where are you?"

"At the hotel. Maybe fifteen minutes away."

"Does Ryan know all the details?"

"He does. I paid him a dollar so he's officially my attorney now, so if he tells anyone this confidential information he's in trouble with the law."

"I guess that's good enough. Give us another hour and we'll start packing up."

After I'd hung up, I turned back to Ryan. "We're on. Why don't you come by around three?"

"Great. See you at the B&B."

I left him to settle the bill and walked out to the parking lot, when I remembered the phone message. I returned the call and Frances Carter answered quickly.

"Kate. I've got a terrific pile of stuff, if you want to stop by and see it. Don't worry, I won't keep you long, but I thought you might want to work out some sort of strategy to use it, maybe for promoting your project."

"I'm going that direction right now, and I'd love to see what you've got. Be there in ten!"

I headed out of the parking lot toward downtown Asheboro. I found a parking space in front of the newspaper building and went up the stairs quickly. I found Frances seated at a table at the back with a foot-high stack of yellowed newsprint in front of her. She waved vigorously when she saw me. She was still the only person in the room.

"Thanks for coming back, Kate. When I saw how much we had I got excited. Nobody's looked at this stuff for a long time. Not even the microfilm version, much less the digital records."

"I'm impressed. Can you give me a thumbnail sketch of what you've got?"

"I'd say fifteen percent is social — you know, Henry's marriage and some activities for the couple. I must say, reading between the lines, poor Mary was either pathologically shy or always sickly. You know anything more?"

"Not really. From what I've seen from his home, Henry didn't file away any personal correspondence, but they were sharing the house anyway, so why would they have written to each other? I'm guessing her death devastated him, because he seemed to change after she was gone. Poor man."

"Well, the other eighty-five percent was about the factory, which employed most of the men in the town, the ones who weren't farmers. There are a lot of descriptions about what he made, where his shovels were sent, even some profiles of his outstanding workers. And it wasn't for his own glory, either. He was proud of what he'd built, and what it meant to the town. For someone I never met, I kind of like old Henry."

"I know what you mean. He built an amazing house, and I have to wonder how much of that was to make his wife happy. Can I take a look at the printouts?" I held out a hand.

"Sure. These aren't the originals anyway, although we do have them. Help yourself."

I leafed through a portion of the papers. They included a surprising number of photographs which looked like they had come from the local paper. "When did the paper start using photographs?"

"Oh, around 1885, I think. Our little paper was well ahead of its time, for a small local. I've often wondered if Henry somehow paid for us to upgrade."

"That's great." I shuffled through some more, and at the sight of one I went still. *Could it be?* I slid it back toward Frances. "Is that Henry on the left?"

"I think so. He's in a lot of the pictures."

"Do you recognize the man on the right?" I asked carefully.

Frances took another look. "I think that's Thomas Edison. Henry knew him slightly. I'd have to dig up the original article, but I think the story was that Edison was traveling around flogging whichever invention he was working on at the moment, and he happened to pass through this part of the world. Don't know how the picture came about, though."

"May I keep this copy?"

"Sure, I can make plenty more, thanks to our digital files."

I *so* wanted to stay and keep hunting, but I was supposed to meet Ryan at the house shortly. "Frances, this is wonderful, and exactly what I need. Thank you for putting this together for me. And I'll look forward to coming back, since I feel like I've only scratched the surface. If you find anything else interesting, please set it aside for me."

"Happy to be of help. Not a lot of people ask me to help anymore. I miss it."

I laughed. "I'll give you as much as you can handle, I promise. Maybe we can even get your high schoolers involved. Thank you!"

I all but skipped down the steps to my car. I'd seen enough photographs of Edison to recognize the man when I saw him, and the date was right. So I now had a photo of Henry and Edison together at the right time, in the right place. Maybe our theory wasn't so crazy after all.

# 24

I sped back to the B&B as quickly as the law would allow, not that it was very far. I think I had a silly grin on my face all the way.

I felt ridiculously psyched. Here the three of us reasonably intelligent, experienced professional adults had sat down and cooked up a pie-in-the-sky theory about something that had happened well over a century earlier, based on the feeblest of hints, and I had just lucked into a tangible piece of evidence — the picture — that greatly increased the odds that we had been right. The timing was right, and such an exchange fit what we knew about Edison. And would someone kill Zach unless there was something important at stake? Tangible proof of Asheboro's part in the fledgling electric industry would certainly qualify.

I knew this was only a baby step forward, but after so many frustrations and guesses I was happy to take what I could get. And I'd made a new friend and contact in town; Frances Carter and her newspaper could be a real asset in boosting my plan, and could even attract more townspeople to participate. What about a Memories column, where people could talk about what they remembered or what their parents and grandparents had told them about the old Asheboro? What about a regular role at the paper for the high school kids? Those who planned to go to college could use a public service credit on their application. And they could handle the computer stuff that Frances couldn't, since they probably didn't care about learning how to set type (about which I knew almost nothing). Plenty of possibilities!

I beat Ryan back to the B&B. Josh's car was still parked in front. I didn't see Eric's. Speaking of Eric, there was something odd about that guy. Maybe he was going through some sort of emotional crisis and wanted nothing more than to be left alone to commune with nature — or with Civil War graves — which might explain why he was avoiding Carroll and me. Or maybe he had a terminal illness and was looking for burial possibilities. Not my business anyway. I wasn't even his hostess — I was just letting him use a bed in the house where I was staying that happened to belong to an old friend of mine who also happened to be Eric's old friend — an example of small-town networking. Nothing like the hotel business I was used to.

I parked behind the building and let myself in. "Where is everybody?" I called out.

"Library!" I heard Josh's voice call back. I found Carroll and Josh sprawled on wing chairs and looking very pleased with themselves.

"You found what you were looking for?" I asked.

"We think so," Josh said. "I'm going to need to check out some other sources, but it looks promising."

I dropped in a third chair. "Well, I found something too. This town has had a one-horse newspaper since the dawn of time, but they've kept all their old records, and they were even digitized a few years ago. The woman who runs the paper now has been there forever and knows what's what. I asked her to find what she could about Henry and the factory and such. Look what we found!" I handed Josh the print of Henry and Edison.

Josh looked at it and did a double take.

"Is that — ?"

"It is," I said triumphantly. "And the date fits."

Josh passed the page to Carroll. It didn't take her long to make the connection. "Wow. And the original newspaper is still on file somewhere?"

"So Frances said. Who knows what else is buried in those records?"

"Fantastic," Carroll added. "So, what now?"

"Ryan is on his way over here, and he said he'd take the boxes we brought from the factory to his office, where they have a very large safe. One or more of us should go with him and the documents. For the moment we're sort of the official custodians of the documents, along with the town. And since I hired Ryan" — I made air quotes — "he doesn't need to know all the details, and we have him on board if we need a lawyer, which seems likely."

"Damn, I hadn't even thought of that," Josh said. "But what I'd be most useful for is authenticating any claims. It may be a murky mess, because Edison churned out patents and often sold them and squabbled with most of his major competitors."

"One step at a time," I told him. "I think I can market this meeting of Edison and

Henry without absolute proof. At least we can show that Henry and Edison knew each other, which should be worth something. If nothing else it would elevate Henry's status in the business world of the day."

I heard a key in the front door and I assumed it was Ryan, but I was surprised to see Eric walk in. "You look like you've been busy," he commented.

"Oh, we have," I said quickly. "Are you just stopping by, or do you have more sightseeing to do?"

"I haven't decided. I'd forgotten how much energy being a tourist requires."

I had noticed that he looked kind of tired. "There should be two categories of vacations: sightseeing and just plain relaxing. What have you seen so far?"

"I'm ashamed to admit that I never toured Gettysburg before this week, even though I live relatively close. That's an interesting experience."

We all chatted aimlessly while I tried to work out what to do: Ryan was due to arrive any minute — in fact, after my detour to the newspaper, I had expected him to arrive before I had — but I didn't want Ryan to talk about why he was here. But if Ryan walked in, then carried out several large old boxes, Eric was sure to be curious. I wasn't quite sure what their relationship was, but if Ryan called Eric a friend he would be likely to mention his task. Maybe I needed to intercept Ryan at the door.

I hoped that Josh and Carroll weren't about to blab about what we were working on. I'd tried to impress on them the need for discretion when mentioning the new Barton papers, but I wasn't sure if they'd taken me seriously. Surely they would recognize that Eric didn't need to know about what had been in Henry's attic, much less the factory? But the two of them were so giddy with what they'd found that I didn't trust them to think before they spoke.

Where was Ryan? He should have been here by now. I *really* needed to call Detective Reynolds.

I was supposed to be making neutral conversation with Eric, right? I was getting tired of trying to navigate the murky waters of "who knows what now?" Maybe it was time to simply jump in.

"Eric, what's the company you work for? Mid-Atlantic?"

"Yes, that's true. I've been with them for quite a while. We've been producing power for over a century, including for this region, and we've grown with the times."

"That must be interesting these days, with

more and more options becoming available — solar, wind, and so on. And demand just keeps growing, doesn't it?" I knew I was babbling, and Josh and Carroll were staring at me oddly. Eric just looked bemused.

Carroll joined in the fun. "And you grew up in Philadelphia and live in Delaware now. Do you know Baltimore at all?"

"Only in a professional capacity. Mostly short trips, then home again. Why the sudden interest?"

Our questions were innocuous — and we'd been careful not to share too many details, so I realized that Ryan might not have known the connections between Henry Barton's papers and local power generation history. I certainly hadn't until I found myself in the middle of the mess. It couldn't be a coincidence, could it?

Luckily Ryan finally arrived and let himself in. I hurried out to the hall to stall him.

"Sorry, Kate; I got sucked into a business call and it just kept going," he apologized.

"Ryan, Eric is here," I said in a low voice.

"Great! I haven't seen a lot of him this week."

"Please don't talk about the Barton papers, okay?"

"Why not? Isn't that why I'm here now? Kate, you're acting pretty odd. Is something wrong?"

"I . . . don't know. Maybe. Can you trust me on this?"

"If that's what you want. Can we go in now?"

"Sure." I led the way into the library.

"Hey, Josh, Carroll," Ryan greeted them heartily. "Eric, where have you been hiding? I thought I'd see more of you this trip."

"Just out and about, Ryan. I had no clear idea how much ground I'd have to cover to see all the sites I wanted to see. Were you looking for me? You could have called my cell."

"No, I'm here to do a favor for Kate. Where's the stuff you wanted me to see, Kate?"

"Come on, I'll show you." I all but dragged him to the kitchen, and then into the pantry, where the boxes of documents were stacked on the floor.

"Kate, are you feeling all right?" Ryan asked.

"Sure, fine." If paranoia was the new normal. "Let's get Josh to help you carry this stuff out to your car."

When we went back to the parlor, Josh agreed willingly. "No problem. You need to get back to your office, don't you, Ryan?"

Ryan was looking more and more confused. "Hey, I've got time for a drink."

Stalemate. I wanted Ryan on the road to his office — the one with the nice safe — with the loot, and he was preparing to settle in for a cozy chat. Not good. Josh understood the problem, but Ryan wasn't paying any attention to him.

I hoped Carroll was still swapping Philadelphia stories with Eric. While Josh and Ryan shuttled the boxes out to Ryan's car, I called Detective Reynolds, praying that he wouldn't be in his office. When he answered I breathed a sigh of relief. "Detective, I have some new information for you. Could you possibly come over to the bed-and-breakfast in Asheboro now?"

He was silent for a long moment. "Is this important?"

"Yes, I think it is. Can you trust me on that?"

"All right. I'll be there within the hour."

"Thank you. I'll explain when you get here."

"I'll count on it."

# 25

After I'd hung up, I went back to the library. Ryan and Josh had not come back from loading the car. "Is it too early to open a bottle of wine?" I asked nobody in particular. "Eric, have you seen enough battlefields for one day?"

"I think I'd prefer coffee, if you don't mind. But I think I've seen enough for today."

"I'll make the coffee," Carroll said, jumping out of her chair and heading for the kitchen.

That left Eric and me on our own. He did look tired — not as though he'd been enjoying his vacation. "Were you comparing notes on Philadelphia with Carroll?" I asked, just to make conversation.

"We were. She's younger than I am, so her memories are different. But you know the city as well, don't you?"

"Yes, although it's been several years since

I spent any time there. I was working for a hotel, so I didn't get as much time to sightsee as I might have liked. I guess the same was true for me when I worked in Baltimore."

"So you're making up for it in Asheboro?"

"You mean, digging into the details of the place? Yes and no. I grew up here, but I wasn't particularly interested in the past. Now I see things differently. I feel like there's more I can do to have an impact on the town here, rather than at a big urban hotel, and if I'm lucky, I can help rescue the town."

"I admire your courage," Eric said. "Striking out in a new direction, and helping other people."

Ryan and Josh came back, and I wondered what if anything they'd talked about as they'd loaded the boxes into Ryan's car. It was getting increasingly difficult to remember who knew what, not to mention what was fact and what was hypothesis.

The doorbell rang, and I said brightly, "Who could that be?" as I went to answer, hoping it would be Detective Reynolds. I opened the door to find . . . Alison? What was she doing here?

"Hi, Alison," I said, my mind racing. "I thought you'd gone home. Looking for something? Or someone?" I asked, blocking the doorway.

"Kate, we need to talk. I have some questions for you," she said, more or less shoving her way past me. She headed straight for the library, and I rushed to catch up. She stopped in the doorway and I all but ran into her.

"Eric?" she said incredulously.

Eric stood up and, in much the same tone, said, "Alison?"

I pushed her into the room. If I hadn't been so confused I would have found the confrontation funny. Eric and Alison knew each other? Ryan knew Eric, but had he met Alison? Josh had met Ryan but knew Alison better than Ryan did — but did he know that Alison knew Eric? Carroll was watching the scene with a half smile on her face while the coffee perked. Me, I was getting a headache. What was the first question I should ask?

"Okay, everyone, sit down," I finally said. "I'm so glad we're all in the same room, because it should save time explaining. Alison, how do you and Eric know each other?"

"We work for the same company. Different departments," she said, her voice tight.

"You mean Mid-Atlantic Power?" I hadn't seen that coming. "Eric, is that right?"

"Yes, it is." He looked troubled.

"Did you know Alison would be here?" I demanded.

Eric shook his head. "No. She didn't tell me. Nor did I tell her I was traveling to Asheboro. Not that she's under any obligation to give me her schedule. It's a large company."

Nobody seemed to want to volunteer anything more, so I pressed on. "So neither of you knew the other one was here. Interesting coincidence. Why don't we figure out what the heck is going on?"

Nobody protested; everybody stared expectantly at me.

"Let me cut to the chase; it'll save time," I said. "I think I can guess why you're here, Eric. The Edison patents. Specifically, the patents that Henry Barton acquired from Thomas Edison." I truly hoped I was right.

"You know about them?" Alison asked incredulously.

*Bingo!* "I do. So do Carroll, Josh, and Ryan. Not only do we know about them, we found them," I said triumphantly. "How do *you* happen to know about them? Have you and Eric been working together to find them? Wait — how did you even know they existed?" This whole line of questioning was more complicated than I thought.

Eric looked at Alison, who avoided his gaze. Then he turned back to me. "Zachary Mitchell came to me and told me he thought they might exist."

That was definitely something I hadn't expected to hear. "You knew Zachary?" From the corner of my eye I saw Alison stiffen. Curiouser and curiouser. But for the moment I was focused on Eric.

"Let me explain," he began. "Mid-Atlantic created an internship program for students several years ago, and I've been managing recruitment for it. Zach was one of the applicants last year. He was a smart kid with a bright future."

"What was he working on for you?"

"I work in corporate finance. MAP is a company that's been in business for over a century, and our older records are rather jumbled, though that's nobody's fault. I asked Zach to spend his time with us putting them in some kind of order and doing some data entry. He reported to me. I believe he started with the earliest records and he was making good progress. He was very eager."

"Would that kind of position have put him in line for permanent employment when he got his degree?"

"We certainly would have considered him,

if he did a good job. I think he was trying hard to prove himself. Anyway, after some time working on the MAP archives, he came to me about something he thought he'd found reference to in the documents. Corporate history claimed that the original company had been founded based on patented inventions from Thomas Edison — that's what all our PR materials say. Zach told me he thought that the original patents might have been filed by Edison, but that he had sold them before MAP supposedly acquired them. Zach thought the legal owner was Henry Barton, whom none of us had ever heard of. Edison was notoriously sloppy about the legal side of things, so that was believable."

Ryan had remained silent, but now he asked, "What did you do about it?"

"Nothing, I'm sad to say," Eric said. "I was particularly busy when Zach came to me with this information, and more than that, I thought the whole idea was farfetched. He'd been a bit overeager to find something, to make his mark. I said something like, 'Thanks a lot, I'll look into it,' and then I shelved it."

"How did Zach react?"

"I don't know. We didn't have much contact at the company — I was fairly senior to him. But after a while I did find time to give the idea some thought, and I realized that if there was any possibility that what he'd said was true, we have a legal obligation to investigate it. I didn't have the time, but I told Alison what Zach had told me and asked her to look into it, since she handles public relations."

All eyes turned to Alison. She looked defiant.

"And what did you do, Alison?" I asked.

"I asked Zach to share what he had found," she said. "I told him Eric was interested in his idea and had asked me to help him follow up. Zach did some more digging and came up with the Asheboro connection."

"And that was when you came to Asheboro?" I asked. "Did you and Zach come together?"

"Hang on," Josh interrupted. "That's not what you told me, Alison. You said you were working on a presentation and wanted to pick my brain for information. You never mentioned Barton or MAP."

"Josh, you were living at the Barton estate!" Alison protested. "It was the perfect opportunity for me to find out local details. And the conference was a legitimate cover story — you've probably already looked it up. But when I arrived you and your friends were in the process of shifting all the documents around, so I couldn't exactly dig through them. And I didn't want to talk about the patent problems until I knew more."

"But Zach got here first, didn't he?" I asked. "He was in Asheboro, and he knew about the documents. You weren't working together at all, were you, Alison?"

She shook her head. "No. He wanted to get full credit for the discovery, and make sure Eric knew who had found it, because he wanted a long-term job. Zach didn't know that Eric had already shared the information with me and I was working on it. I didn't guess that he'd keep looking — I thought that when Eric had downplayed the idea, Zach would forget about it. And then we just happened to run into each other on the street here, and we each had to explain why I was in Asheboro, and I suggested that we work together."

I turned to Eric. "Were you aware of any of this?"

"No. Neither Zach nor Alison shared their plans with me."

"Then why are *you* in Asheboro? Did you know either of them was here?"

Eric shook his head. "You must think I'm

stupid. I have in fact known Ryan for years, and it seemed like a good time to visit. And I really am interested in Civil War history. I wasn't here to dig around for patents or anything else. When I arrived I learned about the Barton mansion, and something clicked, so I started to do a little more research. To be honest, I'd never looked into the history of MAP, and I hadn't realized there were any local connections here. I'm sorry, Ryan; I didn't plan to take advantage of you."

It struck me that nobody had mentioned one very important point. "Eric, do you know that Zach is dead?"

"What?" Eric exclaimed. "I never heard that."

"You told me you'd overheard someone say someone had been found dead in the town library," I reminded him. "That was Zach."

It took Eric a few moments to pull himself together. "I don't watch the local news much, or read local papers. I didn't get any calls from the home office either — maybe they didn't know, or didn't think Zach's death mattered. How could I have been aware of his death?"

Actually, his excuses sounded reasonable — I couldn't remember the last time I'd read a paper or watched the television news since I'd arrived in town. "The police who are investigating didn't want to release his name publicly until they knew a bit more, although they verified that he was not local. It's likely that nobody connected him with you or your company." I swallowed. "I was at the library the day before his death, and he stopped by and told me that he was looking into his family's genealogy, which was a good cover story but we know now it wasn't true. He died at the library later that night, and Carroll and I found the body the next morning. So you can see why it seems suspicious that Zach and Alison and you all show up in Asheboro at the same time, apparently looking for the same thing. Have either you or Alison talked to the police?"

"Not me," Eric said. "Alison, why didn't you update me on your research?"

Alison shook her head vehemently. "Eric, you told me to look into it, and that's what I've been doing. I didn't think I had anything important to report to you. I don't know what you said to Zach, or whether you'd told him you asked me to help, but he didn't contact me."

"But once you got here, you ran into each other," I said. "It's a small town. And you said you agreed to work together."

"Yes, as colleagues. We weren't friends. Nominally Zach reported to Eric. I'm in a different department. But Eric thought I might have some insights into the situation, since I handle public relations, among other things, which is why he brought me in. Or maybe he thought Zach was making things up and wanted me to check. We didn't talk about it in any detail."

I looked around the room. Everybody looked tired and confused, but I had a gut feeling that at least one of them was lying. Zach had been killed in the library, although I'd been careful not to mention he'd been murdered, saying only that he had died there. Funny — nobody had asked about how he had died. Carroll and I knew that he had not been alone, and had not died accidentally, but I wasn't about to volunteer that information. I refused to accept as a coincidence the fact that three people associated with MAP and who had all known each other through the company had shown up in a tiny town in the middle of nowhere at the same time. One of them had died, so there had to be some connection. The logical conclusion was that this issue of the patents had to be important to one or more of these people, for financial or professional reasons. But who had killed Zach?

My suspect list consisted of Alison, Eric, and maybe Ryan (who as a friend of Eric might be hoping for some hefty legal fees if he was hired by MAP to fix things?). How was I supposed to sort this out? And where was Detective Reynolds? Surely he must have learned something new since we last talked.

My question was answered when the doorbell rang. I jumped up to open the door and found the detective there.

"Detective, I am ever glad to see you. There are some things you need to hear, and not just from me. Please, come in!"

# 26

Detective Reynolds followed me to the library without speaking. He acknowledged those of us he had already met, and then stepped forward. "Let me guess: the newcomers are Eric Harbison and Alison Delcamp?"

"You have been doing your homework, Detective," I told him. "And it appears that they and Zach shared a common motive for being in Asheboro."

"I understand they are all employees of the same company, Mid-Atlantic Power."

He already knew? "Correct! But there's one more fact that you need to know: it appears possible that all of them were searching for patents for some sort of electrical systems that Thomas Edison sold to Henry Barton, which in turn became the foundation for the business we now know as Mid-Atlantic Power. The question of ownership is unclear."

"Ah," Reynolds said. "And this, in your opinion, could be the motive for Zach Mitchell's death?"

"I think it's possible," I told him. "Do you have any evidence that points to his killer?"

"Some." He turned to the group, where everyone was staring expectantly at him. "Why don't you let me summarize what I've learned since the young man's death, and then you can comment?"

After everyone nodded silently, the detective began, "I understand that Zach Mitchell was a student and an intern hired by the company, under the supervision of Mr. Harbison. That information did not appear in any public records, so we had to check with his university. What was he doing for you, Mr. Harbison?"

"I asked him to sort out the company's early corporate documents. He made good progress. Then he came to me and told me that he'd found something he thought might be important. I was not convinced by his description, but I asked Alison to look into it, since it fit better with her job responsibilities."

"Ms. Delcamp, you are an assistant vice president for public relations, right?" Alison nodded. "And you were acquainted with Mr. Mitchell?"

"Only after he had spoken with Eric, and Eric passed the story on to me."

I noticed she didn't mention finding him in Asheboro, but I didn't want to interrupt the detective.

"So you looked into the issue of the patents and determined that it was worth following up, which is what brought you to Asheboro?"

"Yes."

"Were you traveling with Mr. Mitchell?"

"No. I came here on my own to consult with Josh Wainwright on a presentation I planned to make at an upcoming conference, and I was staying in a hotel rather than in town here in Asheboro."

"And you never crossed paths with Mr. Mitchell?"

Alison hesitated, then said, "No."

"Were you familiar with the town library?"

"No. I understand it's closed at the moment."

"Do you know where Mr. Mitchell was staying?"

"No. Why would I?"

"When did you learn that Mr. Mitchell was dead?"

"I heard that someone had died in the library, but I didn't know it was Zach."

"What about you, Mr. Harbison?"

"I heard about *a* death, but until today I didn't know that it was Zach. I've been playing tourist while I was here, and didn't pay much attention to local news."

The detective chose his next words carefully. "Forgive me if this seems intrusive, but were any of you involved in a romantic or physical relationship with anyone else in the group?"

I almost laughed. I decided not to mention that Josh and I were, sort of, but Detective Reynolds already knew that. The only possible pairings were Alison and Zach, Alison and Eric, Alison and Josh (which I thought was unlikely), or possibly Eric and Zach. Or Eric and Ryan. I didn't think any of those made sense. Another thought struck me. "What about alibis for the time of Zach's death, Detective?"

"Which was when?" Eric asked.

"Most likely between midnight and 8:00 a.m. last Wednesday night or, more accurately, Thursday morning."

Eric looked relieved. "Ryan and I were in a bar until it closed on Thursday night. Then I came back here to the bed-and-breakfast to sleep."

I thought I should point out something to Detective Reynolds. "Before you ask, Eric is a very quiet guest — I never heard him come in or leave, so I can't verify when he returned. He did have a key to the place, and the code for the alarm system."

"Duly noted," the detective said. "Ms. Delcamp, what about you?"

"I told you, I've been staying at the hotel a few miles from here. I don't know if they have electronic records of people's comings and goings."

"They do not, Ms. Delcamp. I checked with the hotel where you were registered."

Eric broke in. "How did Zach die?"

"Evidence suggests that he broke in through a side window of the town library and crawled in through it. In that process he somehow tipped the old wooden bookcase over and it fell on him, injuring his skull. He died quickly."

Carroll and I exchanged a glance; we knew that wasn't what Reynolds had told us. Did he have a reason for muddying the waters?

Detective Reynolds looked at each of the members of the group, and we all remained silent. Finally he said, "Have any of you found evidence of the patents in question?"

Finally, something I could answer. "Yes. We believe we found them in the old factory in town, in a safe. That Henry Barton knew Thomas Edison personally is corroborated by articles and photographs in the local newspaper."

"So Mr. Mitchell's assumptions were quite possibly correct."

"We think so."

The detective turned his attention to Eric. "Mr. Harbison, if what you suspect is true, what would be the impact on your company?"

"It could potentially have a significant impact on Mid-Atlantic," Eric admitted. "I'm not a lawyer, but I think we have to look into it. If you're wondering, I have no wish to conceal the documents' existence — I don't want a cover-up."

"Who would benefit if these documents hold up in court?"

We all looked at each other. I know we had all assumed that Mid-Atlantic would suffer, but who stood to gain? Henry had left no heirs. He *had* left his properties to the town of Asheboro, assuming the town would sell them, so did the town stand to gain? That was an intriguing idea, but I didn't have the legal experience to guess.

Reynolds seemed to be on the same page as I was. "Mr. Harbison, if these patents did in fact belong to Henry Barton rather than Thomas Edison, would your company suffer?"

"Probably. It might take years to figure out the legal aspects of their ownership, assuming the evidence survives at all. But that uncertainty might interfere with our current operations and plans."

"To whom would this matter the most?"

"At MAP? Myself, of course. Some other department heads, possibly. And Alison would have to deal with the public aspects."

Detective Reynolds paused for a few seconds before asking quietly, "Mr. Harbison, did you have anything to do with Zach Mitchell's death?"

Eric straightened his back. "No, sir, I did not. I understand why you would see me as a potential suspect, but I'm not a killer. Zach Mitchell was a good kid — smart, hardworking. I would have been happy to hire him when his internship was over. I'm sorry I didn't give his report the attention it deserved when he first presented it to me, and I can understand why he persisted in following up. He was right; it's important."

Detective Reynolds nodded once, and he appeared to be satisfied with Eric's answer. Then he turned to Alison. "Ms. Delcamp, what about you?"

Alison looked like a deer in the headlights for a moment. "What do you mean?"

"Would your job be affected if this question of who owns the patents became public?"

"Eric would have a better handle on that than I would. I would end up managing the public relations aspects, though not the legal ones. The company would need me to provide information to the public. And to investors, and our legal representatives. That's why I would need to know the details, up to a point."

"Then let me ask you this: Would your job have been easier for you if these documents had never been found?"

Alison shrugged. "It's hard to say. This is an unusual problem. But evidently Zach believed they existed. And now we *all* know that they do, although not what they may say or if they're still applicable after so much time has passed."

I couldn't stay out of the discussion. "Alison, you know that Zach was found dead in the library, and I have to assume he was there hunting for the documents we're talking about. Did you believe documents regarding the patents might be there?"

"I thought it was possible, although it's a rather small library. Still, there aren't a lot of choices in this town, are there? I knew you and Carroll were all over the attic of the mansion, going through what was there, and planning to move whatever you found to the library in order to catalog the files. You told us that you met Zach when he came by the library the evening before he died, and I have to assume he was being thorough. I have no idea if he was aware of the factory building or where it might fit among Henry Barton's holdings. I knew of it only because Josh spoke of it as an example of small-town industry from the 1800s. But I would not have assumed there was anything stored there, much less legal documents, after so long."

"Did you and Zach ever discuss any possible documents collections?"

"No. Why would I? I had no idea that Zach was still looking — I assumed Eric had discouraged him. He asked me to look into it only after thinking about it for a while."

It was becoming obvious to me that I didn't understand how a big corporation worked. All right, Zach thought he had found something, but he was a lowly intern, not an employee. It was easy to see why Eric had dismissed his suggestions. It was less obvious why Eric had given it further thought and decided it was worth pursuing. But why ask Alison to look into it?

"Eric, why didn't you just ask Zach to dig

deeper? He was the one who brought you the idea, and he seemed enthusiastic and willing, didn't he?"

"You're right, Kate. He just happened to present his idea to me at a bad time — I was handling several other corporate issues that I thought were more important. After further thought I came to believe his idea was worth investigating, but Zach had limited experience with historic industrialization or even with MAP, so I asked Alison to look into the details. And that's where things rested when you found Zach dead. We had no evidence or confirmation, just an interesting theory."

I glanced at the detective before going on. "Then let me ask this: What would you have done if Zach had found what he was looking for, and they appeared to be valid?"

"Are you asking if I would have silenced him, to protect MAP? I'd like to hope not. And I think Alison could have spun it in our favor, although I hadn't looked at the financial implications."

That fit with my assessment of Eric Harbison's character, based on what little time I'd spent with him, but I wasn't about to assume I was a good judge. I'd ask Ryan sometime, if we ever dug ourselves out of this crime.

The detective jumped in before I could frame another question. "Ms. Delcamp, were you ever inside the library building?"

Alison looked startled. "I stopped in briefly to talk to Josh there. This was my first trip to this area, and Josh told me the library wasn't open at the moment. If I had thought there was some merit to Zach's theory, I might have tried to persuade the town leaders to let me check out the collections, but my own search hadn't gone that far."

"Why didn't you just ask Josh to get you in? Or me?" I asked.

"To be honest, I thought what you found in Henry Barton's attic was a more likely place to look, and I might have asked to see that material once you'd finished moving it. And I was still trying to maintain a low profile, on behalf of MAP, in case this proved to be a dead end."

That seemed to be a reasonable explanation. But I was still troubled. Zach was dead. He had been killed by a falling bookcase. Or had he? Coming in through the side window I could accept. He could not have been seen from the street on that side. He was young and apparently in reasonably good shape. The bookcase had certainly seemed solid, although I hadn't looked at it carefully. But the idea that Zach could have tipped it over onto himself was less than believable. Carroll, Josh, and I had all agreed on that.

Which left me or Eric or Alison or maybe Ryan as the killer. Eric certainly looked physically capable of it, as did Ryan, leaving aside any clear motive. What about Alison? I couldn't guess how strong she was, although she was no frail flower. I certainly couldn't say how cold-blooded she was. What would she gain by killing a short-term intern? Did she have a motive at all? Did anyone else? But Zach was dead, as I knew too well.

Alison looked wary, but she didn't say anything. I studied her, trying to see her as a killer, but it wasn't easy. Until I noted a couple of Band-Aids on her hands and wrists. I couldn't assume they were paper cuts — whatever was under them looked larger than that. Then I remembered the fragments of the broken window, scattered around Zach's body.

I'd been so caught up in my own thoughts that I hadn't realized Josh was talking. "Alison, I never discussed the library in any detail with you. I've used it, and I would have told you that it was highly unlikely that it would have what you were looking for —

it's a small collection, and I don't recall seeing much of anything about the Barton family in it. I recall that you asked about the Clara Barton letters, and I told you they were currently in Philadelphia, and there's no final decision on what to do with them."

"And that's where I came in," Carroll said, breaking her silence. "Kate got in touch with me to go through the rest of the files in the attic, as you know. We're nowhere near finished, but I hadn't seen anything that referred to Henry's business in that material. In fact, Kate and I both noticed that. Henry was apparently a successful businessman and must have made a lot of money, if his home is any indication, but we didn't find anything that pointed to how he made his fortune, which we thought was troubling." She turned toward the detective. "That's why we thought to look in the factory building — it was the only place that seemed logical. In fact, Josh thought he had found some tangible evidence, and insisted we look at the factory. And if we hadn't found anything there, we probably would have dropped the whole subject and moved on to other things. Right, Kate?"

"That was our plan," I agreed. "And we found what we were looking for. Alison, have you cut yourself?"

Alison looked bewildered at my question. I nodded toward her hands, decorated with Band-Aids. "What? No, just some scratches."

Detective Reynolds had been watching the discussion with interest, but my question caught him by surprise. Still, it took him only a moment to figure out why I had asked. "Ms. Delcamp, the evidence at the crime scene included shards of glass scattered around and under the body, on the floor. We assumed they had come from the broken window. We examined them more closely and found that there were traces of blood on some of those shards. We performed basic DNA tests on them, and found they came from a female subject. If I obtain a blood sample from you, will it match the blood on the glass?"

# 27

Alison stared at Detective Reynolds, her face pale. She glanced briefly at Eric, who looked confused. Finally she said, "Yes."

I felt like my brain was spinning in my skull. I was having trouble putting together a mental image — or an explanation — of Alison whacking Zach's head, shoving a bookcase on top of him, and scattering bits of glass around his bleeding body. How? And why?

Alison straightened her back and lifted her chin. "He wasn't supposed to be there."

"At the library, you mean?" Detective Reynolds asked. "Was he the one who broke the window?"

"Yes." Alison didn't elaborate. "He did break in that way."

"But he wasn't the one who tipped over the bookcase, was he?" I said gently.

Detective Reynolds sent me a stern look before saying, "It was not the bookcase that killed him. It was a blow to the back of his head. Was that your doing, Ms. Delcamp?"

"I think I'd like a lawyer," Alison replied, and then fell silent.

Ryan also stood up. "My firm stands ready to represent Eric, if there are any legal ramifications. But I decline to represent Ms. Delcamp. Eric is a long-standing friend of mine, and I cannot see him murdering an intern over some old documents."

The detective nodded once. "Ms. Delcamp, I'll have to ask you to come with me." Alison didn't answer, but stood up and headed toward the front door with the detective without looking back. Apparently she didn't see the need to discuss any of her actions to the rest of us.

"I'll see you out," I said quickly, and trotted after them.

Outside it was dark and quiet. "Thank you," I said quietly, once Alison was settled in the car.

Detective Reynolds turned to face me. "For what? You were right, and I respect your judgment. Although I'm sure I'm still missing some pieces of the puzzle."

"If Alison won't tell you, I can fill you in later. But I guess I mean, thank you for confirming my gut instinct."

"Did you really find the documents?"

"Yes, we did. It was a group effort."

"Are you taking precautions to keep them safe?"

"Of course. Ryan is going to take them to his law firm, which has a really big safe. And Josh and Carroll will be working on verifying their authenticity. Don't worry — none of us is talking to the press." For now, at least, but I was already mulling over how to use this story to the town's advantage, whether or not the patent tale held up in the long run.

"I'm glad to hear it. Good night, Kate. Try to stay out of trouble, will you?"

"Of course I'll try, but it keeps finding me. Good night — and thanks."

I watched as he pulled away with Alison, then I walked slowly back to the building. Right now I wanted nothing more than to sleep, but I had a feeling the day wasn't over yet. Our gathering had collapsed like a punctured balloon after Detective Reynolds left with his suspect in tow, but there were still a lot of loose ends.

Once inside, I saw that Eric still looked stunned.

"Eric, you and I need to talk," Ryan said, looking kind of grim. "I know you've got to be exhausted, but Reynolds doesn't play games. It can wait until tomorrow but not any longer, so get some sleep."

Eric nodded. "This detective seems to be a decent guy."

"From what I've heard, he is," Ryan said.

"I agree," I added.

Ryan nodded at me, then said to Eric, "I'll call you in the morning."

"Fine," Eric said.

"Carroll? Do you have to be back in Philadelphia any time soon?" I asked.

"Heck, no," she said firmly. "I want to start digging through all those lovely documents at the library."

I faced Ryan. "You'll be taking the factory documents back to your office, right?"

"What? Oh, right. Yes. They're even more important now."

"The documents are in your car, right? You want to take them to your office now, or would you rather drag them back inside and deal with them in the morning?"

"Door number one works for me. Eric, will you be staying here tonight?"

"Do you mind if I do? Maybe I'm not directly responsible for the whole mess with the documents, but I could have handled things better. And maybe Zach Mitchell would still be alive."

"It's not your fault, Eric," I told him. "And it was Zach's idea to break in — not a good decision on his part. You know, I hadn't realized how important these pieces of old paper are to some people, and not just for the money they might bring."

"Kate, we'll have to talk too," Ryan said, "but I need to get Eric squared away first. Tomorrow or the next day, okay?"

I nodded wordlessly, and Ryan left. I heard his car start out and pull away. That left me, Eric, Carroll, and Josh, in various states of bewilderment.

Eric looked . . . sad. He'd been too busy at first to look closely at Zach's information, and now Zach was dead, killed by a corporate colleague. Eric hadn't done anything wrong, but I'd guess he was blaming himself for the whole sorry mess. "I'll see you in the morning," he said, and trudged toward the stairs.

One down, three to go.

Carroll looked almost pleased; she hadn't been involved in this whole problem very long, so she didn't really have a personal stake in it. "Can I go to bed now?" Carroll asked plaintively.

"Sure, fine," I said as I waved her away. "Tomorrow is another day."

Carroll snorted, then went up the stairs.

Josh looked annoyed, probably because he knew that Alison had played him. At least he hadn't given away any information of significance. No doubt he was embarrassed that Alison had pulled the wool over his eyes, but he'd done no harm.

"Josh?" I said, looking at him.

"I'm staying here tonight," he informed me. "We should be celebrating. We found what we were looking for."

"Amazing." My brain was rapidly shutting down. I needed sleep, and time to think through what had happened and what it might mean. "Cordy might have left some champagne, but I don't think I'd make it through one glass. Let's save the celebration for later."

What had happened? We'd solved a murder. Not the best advertising for my capabilities, unless I decided to make Asheboro the scene of a mock-murder investigation, staged once or twice a month. I'd heard of such things. Not exactly historical, unless Henry Barton turned out to be a killer. Stranger things had happened, although I kind of liked Henry, based on what I'd learned about him recently. He seemed to have been a very private man; he hadn't set out to make lots of money with his electric experiments but he must have enjoyed creating them. He apparently had loved his wife — had he tailored his social life to accommodate her ongoing illness, whether physical or psychological?

How would the town react to what we now knew? What could we do with the old factory building? Make it a monument to Henry's industry? Did the town stand to earn any money if money for the patents ever changed hands? That could make a significant difference, both to the town and to my plans, but I wasn't about to count those chickens. That could prove a thornier problem than figuring out who owned the patents.

I didn't have to decide anything tonight, did I?

Josh dropped in a chair adjacent to mine. "Well done, Kate," he said.

"What did I do?"

"Found the hidden treasure," he replied.

"Hey, you did as much as I did. Great teamwork, though. Do you have any interest in the papers, Josh? Maybe a book, or at least a nice monograph? Henry's story does fall in your area of expertise."

"I haven't thought that far ahead. But old Henry does sound like an interesting character."

"You think so? I mainly feel sorry for him. From what we've learned recently, he was smart and hardworking. He definitely had good taste. He was something of a visionary, since he saw the potential for developing electric systems. I'm going to guess that he loved his wife, although I don't have a handle on her personality yet. I wonder if they couldn't have kids, or if they chose not to."

"Sounds like a novel, not a historical recounting," Josh commented.

"Maybe. But I'm coming to feel that I know them as people. I can't believe that I lived in Asheboro for half my life and never knew the first thing about them, except that there was a big house that was really nice."

Josh was silent for long enough for me to wonder if he'd fallen asleep, but when I looked over at him, he seemed to be studying me. "What?"

"Do you and Ryan have something going?"

"Not for the last two decades, and I'm fine with that. What, was he staring at me like a lovesick cow when I wasn't looking?"

"No, nothing like that."

"I'm glad to hear it. I think we're going to need him as a lawyer when and if this whole project goes forward."

"You don't think it will?"

"I'm not sure. Is finding two bodies a good or a bad thing?"

"That I can't tell you," Josh said. "But if you get any headlines, grab them and run with them. As long as you put the right spin on the story."

"Either that or we aim for a Halloween ghost party at the mansion."

I was almost too tired to think. Finally I said, "What about you, Josh? Won't your house-sitting contract be up in a couple of months? And don't you have a prestigious academic job waiting for you in the big city?"

"Yes, to both. But if there's hay to be made of the Henry Barton story, it might require a bit of travel, back and forth."

I filed that away for later reflection. "Will there be a market for a book like that? Or maybe I should ask, do you know a publisher who would go for it?"

"Maybe."

"Don't forget to look for some nice pictures. People love old pictures."

"I'll make a note of that."

I struggled to stand up. "I need some sleep. Wherever Henry is now, he must be rolling over in his grave. I should be making plans, but I don't even know where to start."

"The whole mess will still be there in the morning," Josh pointed out. "Unless Mid-Atlantic decides to make a stink. I don't think that's their best strategy, but we'll have to wait and see."

"I hope Eric will keep a lid on things, at least until the legalities are sorted out."

"I think he will. He seems to be a fair man."

"I hope so. Ready to go up?"

"Definitely."

# 28

By the time I got downstairs the next morning, Carroll was long gone. She'd left a note saying, "Gone to library. I'll be back sometime."

I envied her. She had a task that she loved to occupy her mind and her time. Me, I didn't know what to do with myself. I thought briefly about calling Lisbeth, to catch her up on all the events of the last few days, but I thought I should wait until the police had officially cleared Eric (which I assumed they would do) and whatever news was going to come out, had come out. Then I would have to explain to the town of Asheboro what had happened, and we all could figure out where to go from here. After a second cup of coffee I realized that after the herd of guests I'd had over the past couple of days, there probably wasn't a clean sheet or towel to be had, so I might as well start washing. Then food shopping.

Then maybe a nap.

Josh meandered into the kitchen, looking only half-awake. "Coffee?"

"Of course. On the stove."

He managed to find the stove and helped himself.

It was past noon when I was folding the last of the towels in the basement and heard the doorbell. I almost chose to ignore it: What if it was the press? Or more police? Or some clueless person who was looking for a room for the night? I didn't want to talk to any of those. But in the end I decided to be a responsible grown-up and answer the door. I was surprised to see Eric.

"May I come in?" he asked tentatively.

"Of course. So, they didn't arrest you?"

"No, I seem to be in the clear. Except for a lifetime of guilty memories. Maybe I should have handled things better."

"Water under the bridge, Eric. You got tossed into a difficult situation, one that kept changing about every ten minutes. You did the best you could. Come on in."

He followed me into the kitchen, and nodded to Josh before helping himself to coffee. Clearly it was time to make more.

"Anything I need to know?" I asked.

He sat at the kitchen table, and I sat down across from him. I was surprised when he began talking before I could. "This morning Ryan and I covered the basic legal aspects of this patent issue. I haven't heard from the detective, so I can't say what's going to happen to Alison — apart, of course, from losing her job at MAP. But then I got to thinking . . . there are legal considerations, of course, but there are also other issues. Some of them involve you, and Asheboro."

"In what way?"

"I think we have enough information now to say that there is a good reason to believe that Henry Barton has some claim on some of the patents from before 1900, although it will take some digging to figure out which. MAP has employees who can do that research, or Carroll or Josh could find someone with a particular interest in that kind of history. But whatever the truth is, I don't want to see Mid-Atlantic get dragged into this. According to what Ryan told me, Henry left funds to sustain his holdings in Asheboro until the town could sell them, which never happened. Then your local bank president stole those funds, which leaves the town in a hole.

"Ryan also explained what you're hoping to do here, or at least, what you had planned before all the trouble started."

I was almost amused that he considered two murders and an embezzlement no more than trouble. I had to wonder if Asheboro would consider me bad luck and drive me out of town. It took me a moment to focus on Eric again.

"Kate, I admire your vision for this town, but it won't be easy to accomplish, as I'm sure you realize. What's more, I'm fairly sure that Asheboro is not in a financial position to take MAP to court over the rights to the patents and the income they've generated in more than a century. I'd rather not open that can of worms. So I'd like to propose an idea."

"I'm listening," I told him, trying to sound encouraging.

"Good. I would like to see both the town and MAP get ahead of this story. Mid-Atlantic would publicize that your Henry and Thomas Edison collaborated — once we've hired a replacement for Alison — to make possible a major step forward in regional electrification, which has survived even into the present."

"You'd give Henry Barton a share of the credit? In terms of publicity, that could be a big boost for my Asheboro project."

"Yes, and he deserves it. In light of that, Mid-Atlantic would agree to collaborate in the creation of a historical center of some sort in Henry's factory building."

Was he saying what I thought he was? "When you say 'collaborate,' do you mean that your company would provide funding for this center?"

"A reasonable amount, yes, and Mid-Atlantic's name would be associated with the building, along with Henry's. I know you haven't given any thought to what to do with the factory building, so you have no budget in place, but that can be worked out later. I promise you we would be fair — maybe some sort of dollar-for-dollar match, for funds that you and Asheboro raise for this purpose."

My mind was racing, and I didn't know where to start. I didn't even know if I was empowered to accept such a proposal or negotiate terms, since there was no official organization in place, but I wasn't about to say no. "So let me get this straight, Eric. Capital funds from MAP to build out the factory would cost your company far less, in both tangible and intangible terms, than mounting a long and complicated lawsuit?"

"That's correct, and Ryan agrees, subject to some further research. But I would make sure that Asheboro does not get cheated, nor would Mid-Atlantic drag its heels. To be honest, the company does set aside funds for public service projects, and this would fit well."

"Have you talked this over with your company?"

"Not yet, but I think I can make it happen. And I understand that Ryan has offered to represent you and the Asheboro project. There will no doubt be plenty of paperwork involved in setting up the right legal entities, and you would need a management staff and such, but I believe we can do it, working together."

Eric was way ahead of me on the corporate side, but I did not want to look a gift horse in the mouth, and I believed that working together we could make the Barton Factory Museum or whatever we chose to call it a reality, one that would serve everyone's interests. I took a deep breath.

"Eric, I think that is a wonderful idea. Let's find out what needs to be done to get started. We need to set up a meeting with Ryan."

"I'm glad you like it. But let me add that while I have no legal responsibility for Zach Mitchell's death, I will always harbor some sense of guilt. I should have taken him more seriously. I look on the factory project as a form of compensation. And I promise that I will see this through."

"Eric, I look forward to working with you."

He smiled. "I'm glad to hear it. Given what has happened over the past few days, I really need to get back to my office and inform the board and senior employees what has happened. I don't know what your time line is, but this process will take time. But as soon as I get the go-ahead from the board, I'll send you the details and you can present them to the town. Can I assume they will accept our plan?"

Actually, I had no idea. "Eric, there are a lot of parts to this puzzle, and the factory is only one part of it. While I'm eager to get started, I realize that there are things that have to happen first, like setting up a nonprofit organization to manage all of this, because I can't do it alone. And I need to recruit people. And not least, I need to convince the shop owners in town that this can work for them, which may not be easy. What we don't want is a museum in an old building in the middle of nowhere. But I think we can coordinate our efforts. We both need some setup time, and we need to talk to a lot of people. Why don't we set a date to hold a special meeting with the town council and anyone else who wants to attend so that we can present out concept together?"

"That sounds good. Say the beginning of July?"

"I think that could work. And maybe we can take them on a tour of the Barton mansion, because most of them have never seen it, and I think it can be another important part of the puzzle."

"That sounds perfect." He stood up. "I'd better get going, but I promise I will keep in touch, and I hope you will too."

"Of course. And thank you for agreeing to work with us, rather than fighting us on this. It's going to make a big difference."

Before leaving, Eric handed me his keys to the B&B. Then he collected his travel bag from the hall, and went out the door.

Carroll slipped into the room. I hadn't heard her arrive. Had she been eavesdropping? "Wow!" she said. "That sure was interesting."

"Did you hear all of it?" I asked her.

"More or less. I didn't want to interrupt. It's a great offer, if it all works out."

"You're right — it is. But I'm not going to start counting chickens yet."

Then Josh spoke up. "Do you know, if all this works out, we've just changed the history of technology in this region?"

"Are you going to write about it?"

"How can I not? I'm already right in the middle of it."

"I don't know where or how to start," I told them. "First I have to convince myself it's real. Carroll, is there something you have to get back to in Philadelphia this summer, or can you stick around long enough to evaluate all the documents?"

"I wouldn't miss the chance to dig into the Barton papers. Maybe I'll change thesis subjects and work on Henry Barton instead."

"Great. You can stay here in the B&B if you want. Josh, is someone going to replace you as caretaker at the mansion, once your sabbatical is over?"

"It hasn't been discussed yet, or at least, not with me. I may need to juggle my course schedule if I want to stay out here, and it is a good place to get work done. And it's not a bad commute. Are you saying you want to see more of me?"

Did I? "Actually, I think I'd like that."

# 29

"I cannot believe it's been only a couple of weeks since I arrived this time," I told Lisbeth as we sat on her patio consuming glasses of cold drinks with lots of ice cubes.

"Two weeks in which you didn't even bother to call me," Lisbeth protested.

"Well, it's been a busy two weeks, what with trying to talk with half the people in town, and find the rest of Henry Barton's papers. Oh, and solve another murder, which resulted in a very nice financial gift."

"You're telling the town about it tonight?"

"At the special council meeting. Yes, but just the bare bones, since there's a lot that hasn't been finalized yet. Still, I think it should give people a boost to hear about it. And somewhere along the line I'm going to need some approvals from townspeople."

"Has Ryan worked out the management structure for you?"

"In a generic way, but at least we'll have a

structure in place. In case anybody wants to offer us more money — they'll want any donation to be tax-deductible, I assume. Nonprofits are not my strong suit, but I'm learning."

"So, no fanning the flames with Ryan?"

"No. That's our past, and I don't think either of us wants to try again. After all, he married Cordy, which is a strike against him in my book. I don't want to follow in her footsteps. But he is letting me use the B&B as a base while I'm here. He'll probably charge it off as an expense, but it's convenient."

"So that leaves Josh."

"Leaves him for what?" I asked, although I had an idea where she was going with her question.

"Oh, come on. Don't you want a love life?"

"Ask me in a year or so, when I've remodeled Asheboro. Right now I don't have time."

"Uh-huh." Lisbeth grinned at me. "So, tonight's meeting. How much are you going to tell people?"

"About the plan for the town? Just the basics, I think. The MAP gift is going to be a big plus, but it will be a while before the factory building is brought up to code. And we still haven't decided where the Barton collections are going to fit. But then, we don't have any other idea for that building. Shouldn't I let the townspeople have a say in it?"

"First you have to get approval for the general plan, before you start construction."

"I know, I know. Sometimes I wonder if I should have stayed in hotel management — it was a lot simpler." I checked my watch. "Is it time to leave for town yet?"

"I suppose," Lisbeth said, stretching before she got out of her reclining chair. "Don't want to be late for your own meeting, and don't want it to run too long. Tonight all you need is a yes vote."

"Frances asked me to come by early. She said she had something interesting for me, so I need to allow a little extra time."

"I hear she's one of your biggest cheerleaders in town. She's just thrilled that somebody is finally interested in local history."

"That's good to hear, since she has most of it in her archives." I stood up too. "Ready?"

"I guess. Phil's out with the kids for a while longer, so my time is my own. We taking two cars?"

"I guess." Lisbeth's house wasn't far from

the town center, but I was headed back to the former B&B and she had to get home.

When we arrived in the auditorium that the town used for meetings, there was a sizeable audience already seated. Editor Frances was waiting outside the door, and when she spotted me she all but dragged me to a private corner.

"What's so important, Frances?" I asked.

She grinned. "I'll give you the short version now, and we can talk later this week. I've been digging through the old newspaper records, and I found something unexpected. Henry Barton did use those patents we talked about, but quietly — and he built an electric system for the town, at cost. He didn't make a big deal of it, and I can only guess that he earned enough from other electric projects to cover it — but he never asked for much recognition for it. I'm sure somebody can find more details, but I thought you'd like to know."

"Frances, that's amazing. He really was quite a man. I sometimes wish I could have known him."

"I know what you mean. Now, get in there and make your announcements."

"Thank you. We'll get together this week."

Maybe it was because of the air-conditioning, but I was glad to see a number of friendly faces in addition to Frances — Ted, who ran the café and whom I'd known since I was a teenager, and Mr. MacDonald, whose family had been running the hardware store in town for decades. They were sitting together, and they all waved cheerfully. I greeted Mayor Skip, and was surprised to see Eric Harbison — he hadn't told me he planned to come tonight. I hoped he'd brought good news.

Mayor Skip waved to me and cleared his throat before picking up the microphone. "Welcome, everybody," he began, "and thanks for coming this lovely summer night. I'll keep things brief, but I wanted to share some important news of Kate Hamilton's Asheboro renovation project. If you all agree, maybe by the end of the evening we'll be calling it the 'New Old Asheboro Project.' "

That produced a few laughs. I was feeling a little panicky, because no one had told me I might need to make a formal speech tonight, even though there were only thirty or so people in the audience.

Mayor Skip went on, "Before I let Kate speak, there are a few other people who wanted to put in their two cents, starting with Eric Harbison, vice president of Mid-Atlantic Power, which is what keeps the lights on in our town. I'll let him explain why he's here."

I had to remember to keep my mouth shut while Eric laid out the broad outline of his company's more-than-generous gift to support the renovation of the derelict Barton Shovel Factory. Nobody asked any questions, and they were generous with their applause. Then Mayor Skip took the podium again and said, "I'd also like to introduce the members of the newly formed Asheboro Store Owners Association — Frances, Ted, and Mac. They've volunteered to oversee the, well, I guess you'd say the undevelopment of the Main Street stores, to take them back to the way they looked in Henry Barton's day. Not that they're old enough to remember it from then" — the audience laughed — "but they do know their history. They'll be working with Kate. And if anyone else wants to step up and volunteer, I'm sure she'd be happy to have your help. If you've got any questions, stop by and talk to any one of them. And if you have any old photos or letters — just about anything about Asheboro — let Frances know so she can copy them for the town's collection."

Skip paused for a moment to clear his throat. "I wanted to make a brief mention about some of the more troubling events of the past month or so. You know what I mean — the unfortunate deaths of Cordelia Walker, who grew up here, and Zachary Mitchell, who was a stranger. Many of you will have known Cordelia and the role she played in this town. You never had the opportunity to know Mr. Mitchell, but he was instrumental in drawing attention to a significant aspect of our history: Henry Barton's role in developing electrical systems in this part of the world. Please don't let their deaths color your image of Asheboro, or maybe I should say, your vision of what Asheboro can be."

There was a smattering of applause. Then the mayor said, "All right, I'll let Kate have her say. Kate, come on up!"

*Gee, thanks, Skip — a little warning might have been nice.* I took a deep breath. "I'm happy so many of you are here tonight. You know by now that I grew up in Asheboro, but I left after high school and didn't look back, until Lisbeth Scott came to me and told me the town was in trouble and asked if I could help. I couldn't say no to her. And I have to say that I got excited about the possibilities of making the Asheboro of today a place where people would want to live and work, and that would also attract people to see what we've done with the place. Skip mentioned some of the snags we've hit, but we've also had some successes — thank you, Eric — and I hope you're as enthusiastic as I am about getting started. If there's anything you want to see in this town — or *don't* want to see, tell me or a member of our new committee. We want to make this a community project, with everybody playing a part. I won't bore you with the details — mainly because we've just started working on them — but I look forward to working with all of you. Thank you." I left the podium and sat down, my hands still shaking.

Skip marched up to the podium. "Thanks, Kate. We all know that I called this special meeting so we could vote on approving the project, so we can move forward. I think we have a quorum, by the rules for special meetings. All in favor, say aye."

A chorus of ayes broke out.

"Nays?" Skip said.

There was silence.

"The ayes have it, and the project is approved. Can't wait to see what you make of the place, Kate!"

# ABOUT THE AUTHOR

**Sheila Connolly** has published over thirty mysteries, including several *New York Times* bestsellers. Her series include the Orchard Mysteries, the Museum Mysteries, the County Cork Mysteries, and the newest, the Victorian Village Mysteries. She is a member of the Daughters of the American Revolution and the Society of Mayflower Descendants, and owns a cottage in West Cork. She lives in a too-big Victorian in southeastern Massachusetts with her husband and three cats.

The employees of Thorndike Press hope you have enjoyed this Large Print book. All our Thorndike, Wheeler, and Kennebec Large Print titles are designed for easy reading, and all our books are made to last. Other Thorndike Press Large Print books are available at your library, through selected bookstores, or directly from us.

For information about titles, please call:
(800) 223-1244

or visit our website at:
gale.com/thorndike

To share your comments, please write:
Publisher
Thorndike Press
10 Water St., Suite 310
Waterville, ME 04901